Evan Quartermain on the art of being a twin

Sometimes I wonder if my twin brother and I are even related. I've always been "the responsible one," the one with clear-cut goals and plans for my future—Devin was the one who used to get into trouble. But now *I'm* the one in a mess. An anonymous woman left a baby on my desk—a baby that I'm sure isn't mine! Now I have to rely on Devin to find her. Maybe he can also give me some advice on how to handle my next-door neighbor, Claire Walker. She's been so good with baby Rachel, but I'm beginning to wish she'd share some of that TLC with me....

Claire Walker on the art of being a twin

I think Evan is lucky—at least he knows who his brother is. My twin and I were separated at birth; in fact, until recently, I didn't even know she existed. And finding her now may be close to impossible. Growing up, I would have loved to have a sister. I can understand why my daughter, Libby, is becoming so attached to Evan's new charge. To tell the truth, I've gotten a little attached to her myself...not to mention her gorgeous and stubborn daddy, if that's who he is....

Dear Reader,

The holiday season is a time for family, love...and miracles! We have all this—and more!—for you this month in Silhouette Romance. So in the gift-giving spirit, we offer *you* these wonderful books by some of the genre's finest:

A workaholic executive finds a baby in his in-box and enlists the help of the sexy single mom next door in this month's BUNDLES OF JOY, *The Baby Came C.O.D.*, by RITA Award-winner Marie Ferrarella. *Both* hero and heroine are twins, and Marie tells their identical siblings' stories in *Desperately Seeking Twin*, out this month in our Yours Truly line.

Favorite author Elizabeth August continues our MEN! promotion with *Paternal Instincts*. This latest installment in her SMYTHESHIRE, MASSACHUSETTS series features an irresistible lone wolf turned doting dad! As a special treat, Carolyn Zane's sizzling family drama, THE BRUBAKER BRIDES, continues with *His Brother's Intended Bride*—the title says it all!

Completing the month are *three* classic holiday romances. A world-weary hunk becomes *The Dad Who Saved Christmas* in this magical tale by Karen Rose Smith. Discover *The Drifter's Gift* in RITA Award-winning author Lauryn Chandler's emotional story. Finally, debut author Zena Valentine weaves a tale of transformation—and miracles—in *From Humbug to Holiday Bride*.

So treat yourself this month—and every month!—to Silhouette Romance!

Happy holidays,

Joan Marlow Golan
Senior Editor

Please address questions and book requests to:
Silhouette Reader Service
U.S.: 3010 Walden Ave., P.O. Box 1325, Buffalo, NY 14269
Canadian: P.O. Box 609, Fort Erie, Ont. L2A 5X3

Marie Ferrarella

THE BABY CAME C.O.D.

Silhouette
R O M A N C E™
Published by Silhouette Books
America's Publisher of Contemporary Romance

To
Marcia Book Adirim,
pure joy
in the form of
an editor

 SILHOUETTE BOOKS

ISBN 0-373-19264-9

THE BABY CAME C.O.D.

Books by Marie Ferrarella

Books by Marie Ferrarella writing as Marie Nicole

MARIE FERRARELLA

lives in Southern California. She describes herself as the tired
mother of two overenergetic children and the contented wife of
one wonderful man. This RITA Award-winning author is thrilled
to be following her dream of writing full-time.

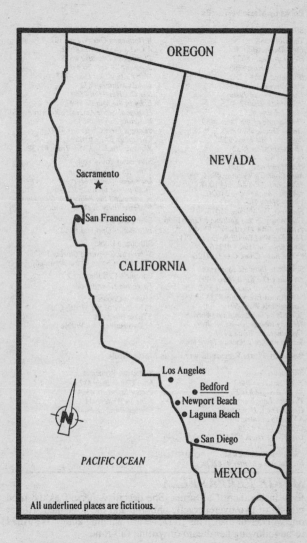

OREGON

NEVADA

Sacramento
★

● San Francisco

CALIFORNIA

● Los Angeles
  <u>Bedford</u>
● Newport Beach
● Laguna Beach
  ● San Diego

PACIFIC OCEAN

MEXICO

All underlined places are fictitious.

Chapter One

"Mr. Quartermain, a lady just dropped off something she said you would know what to do with better than she does."

Evan Quartermain barely glanced up from the monthly status report he was reading. It was an unsatisfactorily written monthly status report, and he meant to chew out the person responsible at the earliest opportunity. He had no time for any games initiated by mysterious women uttering coded messages. Time was something that was in increasingly shorter supply these days.

Why Alma thought the message warranted an appearance from her rather than the usual buzz on the intercom was beyond Evan. He waved a hand in vague dismissal as he circled a particularly daunting and most likely unsubstantiated figure on the spreadsheet that was included with the report. He knew for a fact the statement was incorrect. Didn't people take pride in their work anymore?

"Just leave it on your desk," he instructed. "I'll get to it eventually, time permitting."

Alma had been his secretary for the past four years; Evan had taken her with him as he received each new promotion at what others saw as breathtaking speed. They both knew that time permitted very little for him, other than more work.

She glanced back toward her desk to make sure that what she had left there was secure. "I'm afraid I can't do that."

He sighed, annoyed at being disturbed over what was probably nothing. Keeping a neat desk was an obsession of Alma's. She undoubtedly thought an extra sheet or two left out of place would upset the delicate balance of things. While it was an asset to have such an organized employee, at times he had to admit that it was also a royal pain.

Evan frowned as he circled another figure, pressing progressively harder on his pencil as he went further and further into the report. "Then file it."

"I *really* can't do that."

Her tone had him looking in her direction. His unflappable secretary looked extremely fidgety, and it prodded his curiosity. He never remembered her being difficult.

"And why is that?"

In her own fashion, Alma was very protective of her boss. She went out of her way to spare him any unnecessary annoyances during the course of the day. But there was absolutely no way to shield him from this.

"Because it's a baby."

The pages of the report went fanning through his fingers, settling back down on the desk like so many colored leaves. He had to have heard wrong. "You're joking."

Her thin shoulderblades straightened so far back, they appeared to be touching. "I never joke, sir." With that, she turned on her heel and walked out, leaving the door to his inner office standing open.

But she had gotten his full attention with her announcement. Evan was still staring at the doorway, mystified.

"Then I don't—"

Alma reentered, carrying a baby seat, complete with baby, in her arms.

"—understand..."

Evan's voice trailed off. He didn't remember getting up or rounding the desk, but he must have, because he found himself looking down into the baby's face in utter disbelief. The child was gurgling, and there was a series of interconnecting bubbles going down its chin.

He didn't need this today. Evan raised incredulous eyes to Alma's face. "Whose is this?"

Alma's face was a blank slate as she looked at him. If she had an opinion regarding the matter, it was hers alone and not for sharing.

"Yours, apparently. The note was open." She pointed at the piece of paper that was pinned to the baby's shirt.

It was to Evan's credit that his mouth didn't drop open. There was a note, an actual note pinned to the baby's shirt. This was like something out of one of those B movies from the forties that his brother loved so much. Worse than that, it was surreal.

"I don't have any children," Evan protested.

And he didn't intend to have any. Despite the fact that he came from a fairly large family by present-day standards, the thought of having tiny miniatures of himself and some future wife milling about the house held absolutely no appeal for him. Children were a breed apart, and he didn't begin to flatter himself that he understood anything about that mysterious world. He was a man who knew his strengths and his limitations. Children were part of the latter.

This had to be someone's poor idea of a practical joke, and he couldn't begin to describe his annoyance.

"You do now," Alma said, bringing him back to the present.

The hint of an actual smile on Alma's face testified to the fact that she had always felt Evan Quartermain, latest, as well as youngest, CEO of Donovan Digital Incorporated, couldn't possibly be as completely work oriented as he had led everyone to believe.

Evan didn't care for this breach of loyalty on Alma's part. She above all people should know that if he said something, it was true. Lies and pretenses had no place in his world.

The baby squealed, and Evan's eyes darted back to the round, messy face.

"There's no way," he whispered.

And then, for the first time in Alma's recollection, Evan Quartermain faltered.

"I mean, there's a way, but..." He looked both annoyed and in shock.

Collecting himself, Evan tried to approach the problem logically, as if it were merely another project to be conquered at work and not something with far more devastating consequences. "The woman who brought the baby, what did she look like?"

Like a typical mystery woman, Alma thought. She recited what little there was. "Tall, thin, sunglasses and a scarf." Pointy shoulders rose and fell. "She was in and out before I could stop her."

Evan sighed, running his hand through his dark hair. For whatever reason it was happening, it still had to be a mistake, a gross, ridiculously annoying mistake. There was just no possible way he could be responsible for this gurgling bit of humanity.

Her arms were beginning to ache. Since Evan was making no effort to take the child from her, Alma rested the baby seat on his desk.

"Maybe the note might give you a hint," she suggested. Then, when he didn't remove the paper from the baby's shirt, Alma opened the large safety pin and took it off herself. She handed the note to Evan.

Like someone trapped within a bad dream that refused to end no matter how hard he tried to wake himself up, Evan looked down at the note.

It was addressed to him, all right.

Evan, it took me a long time to find you—otherwise, I would have brought your daughter to you sooner. I've given this six months, but it's just not working out for either of us. You can give Rachel a much better life than I can.

He turned the note over, but there was nothing on the back. No signature, no name, no indication whom the note had come from.

"That's it?" he asked incredulously. He looked at Alma, waiting. There had to be more. "She didn't say anything?"

Alma shook her head. "Just what I said. She wanted me to give you the baby."

There had to be something Alma was forgetting, some minute clue that she didn't realize she had. It was something his brother had told him once. People were always giving away clues about themselves; you just had to listen. Up until this moment, Evan had thought Devin was pontificating from some old Agatha Christie novel, but now he fervently hoped his brother was right.

"Her words," he prodded, "her exact words, Alma."

Since it had happened less than five minutes ago, recalling wasn't a challenge. "'Tell Mr. Quartermain that he'll know what to do with this better than I do,'" Alma recited.

From the frozen, horrified expression on his face, Alma figured that the woman had seriously overestimated Evan's capabilities.

"But I don't know what to do with a baby," he protested.

Evan circled his desk slowly, as if searching for some infinitesimal escape route hidden to the naked eye. And then, slowly, he looked up at Alma, making a last-ditch attempt to reroute the problem, at least temporarily.

"Alma, you're a woman—"

Alma raised her hands. "Stop right there. That fact doesn't necessarily qualify me for anything more than you."

He refused to believe that. "But you must have some sort of maternal instincts—"

"No, I don't. George and I didn't have kids for a reason."

There were more bubbles flowing from the baby's mouth, and she was cooing. Alma reached for a tissue, but rather than wipe the tiny mouth, she handed the tissue to Evan, who took it reluctantly. He dabbed at Rachel's mouth as if it were a stain on the carpet.

Alma frowned at the baby. Her presence was obviously upsetting her boss, and he had work to do.

"Under the circumstances, Mr. Quartermain," she said, already edging her way to the door, "I think your best bet here is family services. Would you like me to get them on the line for you?"

It was a rhetorical question, one Alma was certain her boss would jump at. He didn't disappoint her.

"Yes."

Evan looked down at the baby. Rachel. He rolled the name over in his mind, but it meant nothing to him, nudged no memories to the surface.

That was because she wasn't his, he told himself.

Rachel smiled at him, waving her hands excitedly as she made a noise that sounded suspiciously like a laugh. Probably at his expense. Her eyes were green, a deep, seawater green.

Like his were.

What if…?

"No," Evan said suddenly, looking up toward Alma.

The secretary stopped in the doorway, looking at him with a mixture of surprise and expectation. But she made no further move to her telephone.

Evan tried to think, although for the first time in his life, it was difficult. If he called a government agency into this, there was no telling how much red tape he was going to find himself in. And if, by some strange whimsy of fate, the child did turn out to be his, it would take him forever before he could reclaim her again.

Besides, there was his reputation to think of. He wanted to keep this as quiet as possible.

"Hold off on that," he told her.

"I think you're making a mistake, Mr. Quartermain," she warned.

"Maybe."

Evan tried to put together the scattered pieces in his head into something that made sense. He had a major meeting scheduled for three with Donovan, the president of the company, and several representatives from a Japanese-based firm. That gave him almost four hours to try to get his life into some kind of order.

Like an Olympic lifter psyching himself up to hoist a record-breaking weight, Evan drew in a long breath before picking up the baby's seat. The baby screeched and laughed. He looked, he thought, catching his reflection in the window, like a man attempting to carry a bomb without having it go off.

In a way, he supposed that the comparison was not without merit.

"Alma," he began as he passed her, "I'll be out of the office for a while."

Alma moved farther back, giving him all the room he needed and more. "Are you going to be back in time for your meeting?"

He raised an eyebrow as he spared her a look. "Have I ever missed one yet?"

When she pressed her lips, they disappeared altogether. Her eyes never left the baby. Everything in her body language fairly shouted, *Better you than me.* "No, but you've never had one of those dropped off in the office, either."

"Not a word of this, Alma," he warned sternly. "To anyone. If there's even so much as a hint, I'll know where it came from."

He didn't have to tell her twice. "Understood. What should I say if someone comes looking for you?" she called after him.

He didn't have time to come up with a plausible excuse. There was too much else on his mind. "Make something up. As long as it's not as bizarre as this."

Her small, dry laugh followed him all the way to the elevator. "I'm not that creative."

Neither was he, he thought, looking down into the child's face. Neither was he. Rachel just couldn't be his.

He refused to believe it. He didn't want children, but if he were to have a child, it would be conceived in love, not in error. And he'd never been in love, not even once. He'd wanted to, tried to, but the magic that his brother Devin always talked about had never happened for him.

But then, during their teen years, his twin had fallen in and out of love enough for both of them.

And *he* didn't have one of these, Evan thought sarcastically as he looked down at the child in his arms.

There was just no way she was his.

* * *

His head in a fog, his thoughts refusing to form any rational, coherent ideas, Evan really wasn't sure just how he managed to arrive home in one piece. The only thing he did remember clearly was getting behind the wheel and taking off, then stopping abruptly when he realized that he hadn't strapped the baby seat in properly.

Or at all.

Pulling over to the curb, he fixed that as best he could, fumbling with straps in his blazing red sports car that were never meant to restrain a female small enough to ride in a car seat.

The rest of the drive through the streets of San Francisco was an emotional blur, a rare thing for a man who did not consider himself to be the least bit emotional to begin with. He barely registered the sound of the child wailing beside him.

Over and over again, he kept telling himself that the baby couldn't possibly be his. The number of times he'd been intimate with a woman in the past—what, year and a half?—could be counted on the fingers of one hand. And the number of women he'd been involved with was even less than that. That narrowed down the possible candidates for motherhood, and none of them had had jet-black hair.

He glanced at Rachel. Most babies had little or no hair. She had a mop of it, and it was black as coal.

Like his. Good heavens, like his. Her sudden appearance had rattled him so much, he'd actually forgotten that he had black hair.

The nervous feeling taking hold jumped up several notches on the scale.

In classic denial, he shut away the obvious. She wasn't his.

So what was he doing, acting like a high-school kid who'd been caught trying to blow up the chem lab and was now looking for a way to avoid being expelled? He was a respected member of the business world. This wasn't a matter to be handled by an established bachelor—this was for people who knew what they were doing. Who were accustomed to dealing with abandoned babies.

As he stopped at the red light, Evan entertained the thought of pulling over to the curb and calling directory assistance for the location of the nearest family services office. That would certainly take the matter out of his hands.

Or would it?

There would be questions to answer, questions he didn't have the answers to. And he hated looking like a fool. He'd done enough of that when he was growing up.

And what if word about this got out somehow? The corporation he'd worked his way up in was on the cutting edge of technology, but it was comprised of people whose personal ethics were as old-fashioned as his. There was a new wave of strict morality overtaking the bastions of the corporate world, one that, up until this moment, he had fully appreciated.

It wouldn't look good for him if this was brought to anyone's attention. The members of the board prided themselves on their company's down-to-earth, homespun image, as did Adam Donovan, who had taken a liking to him and a personal interest in his career.

Nothing more homespun than a baby. Unless it was one people were playing hot potato with, he thought cynically.

And despite everything, there was still that tiny, nagging uncertainty in the back of his mind that refused to be completely erased.

What if…?

Well, "what if" or not, first and foremost he had to find someone to take care of this wailing child. Then he would find out who the mother was.

The latter, he forced himself to acknowledge, was right

up Devin's alley. As a private investigator specializing in missing persons, his brother would know how to go about locating this "mystery woman" who was making these false accusations.

But he didn't like having to ask Devin for anything. It wasn't that Devin would refuse him, or even act as if he were being put out—it was just that Evan prided himself on being able to handle anything that came his way, no matter what.

"No matter what" had lusty lungs and was in the process of sucking out every bit of oxygen within the car and turning it into noise. Evan rolled down the window, hoping the street traffic would cut into the wailing and neutralize it.

All his adult life, Evan had gone out of his way to prove how much more responsible he was than Devin. Devin had always been the reckless one, the one who seemed to be without a serious thought. The one his parents had despaired would never amount to anything, not because he wasn't smart enough, but because he didn't apply himself.

Evan's mouth curved in a self-deprecating smile. So why was *he* the one who was being accused of fathering an unwanted child?

Sometimes, the world made no sense.

The open window didn't help. Rachel's cries just rose to the challenge, increasing Evan's feeling of helplessness. The entrance to his development had never looked so good. Not that there were any ready solutions there, but at least he would be out of the crammed confines of the car. His ears were beginning to ring.

"We're here, we're here," he told Rachel, trying to calm her down.

The wailing continued a minute longer, then, as if intrigued by the sound of his voice, Rachel stopped as abruptly as she had started. He felt like rejoicing at the temporary reprieve. It was funny how so little could suddenly mean so much.

"Opera," he murmured, "you should definitely consider a career in opera."

Evan turned into his driveway, not even bothering to use the automatic garage-door opener.

He'd no sooner pulled up his hand brake and turned off the engine than he was laid siege to. Not by the child inside the car, but by the child outside. Out of the corner of his eye, he saw her approaching at ten o'clock. A bouncy four-year-old who was bound and determined, since he'd moved in next door to her and her mother three months ago, to learn everything there was to know about him. He'd already discovered that short, one-word replies did not discourage her. They just led her to ask more questions.

Please, not now, he thought.

"Hi!"

Standing on her toes, Elizabeth Jean Walker hooked her fingers on his open window, all ten of them. Since she was forever eating some candy or other, Evan could just envision what her sticky prints were doing to the highly polished shine on his car.

"You have a baby!" Libby's eyes were huge as she looked past him to the wiggling baby in the car seat. "I didn't know you had a baby!"

"I don't. It's not mine." He put his hand on the latch, then looked at Libby expectantly. "Would you mind stepping back? I need to get out of the car."

Libby danced backward on the points of her toes, her eyes still riveted to the baby. She was pirouetting this week. It went along with her current choice of career—ballerina. Last week, when she had wanted to be a cowhand, she had galloped everywhere she went. "If it's not yours, did you steal it?" There was breathless excitement in each word.

He was glad someone was getting enjoyment out of this.

"No, someone gave it to me." Evan got out and slammed his door.

Without a trace of self-consciousness, Libby stuck with him like a shadow as he rounded the hood to the passenger side. "You mean, like a present?"

Where was this kid's mother? Didn't she know better than to let her little girl run around, harassing neighbors? "No, not exactly."

He stared down at Rachel. Should he take her out of the car seat, or carry her into the house in the seat? He decided on the latter. He didn't want drool on his expensive jacket.

Libby cocked her head, watching him think his problem through. "Whatcha gonna do with the baby?"

"I don't know." He bit off the answer. Evan didn't like feeling as if he was lost, but he still hadn't a clue what to do. There had to be someone he could call, a baby-sitting service that dealt in emergencies. *Something.* He had a meeting to go to, damn it. He didn't have time to stay home and play surrogate father to someone else's child.

Libby wiggled in front of him for a better view of the baby. Swallowing an oath he knew was inappropriate for Libby to hear, he placed both hands on her shoulders and firmly moved her out of his way.

She looked up at him, a sunny expression on her pale face. "Do you need help?"

What he needed right now was for Mary Poppins to come flying down out of the sky. "Yes, I need help." He began working the tangled straps that he'd buckled so haphazardly before while Rachel waved her feet at him, kicking his wrist. "Lots of help. I—"

He looked up, determined to send Libby on her way, but she was already gone.

Well, at least that much had gone right in his life, he thought. The last thing he needed was for Libby to chatter on endlessly in his ear as he struggled to deal with his very real problem.

He should have made a more forceful attempt to talk Alma into helping, he thought, annoyed with himself for giving in so quickly. After all, she was a woman and they had a built-in knack for this sort of thing.

Heaven knew, he didn't.

The baby gurgled happily when he swung her out of the car. "Yeah, you can laugh. You don't have your career riding on a meeting this afternoon. Who *are* you, anyway?"

Rachel answered him by blowing more bubbles.

Evan carried the car seat up to his front door, then tried to do a balancing act while he fished out the keys he'd automatically shoved into his pocket when he'd gotten out of the car.

Through with blowing bubbles, Rachel began to fuss again, trying to eat her foot. All in all, this was not turning out to be one of his better days.

Claire Walker had been staring at the same design on her computer screen for the past ten minutes. Today, apparently, her creative juices had decided to take a hike. No pun intended, she mused, since she was trying to work on a logo for a prominent firm that manufactured athletic equipment.

Nothing was going on in her brain except a mild, familiar form of panic. The kind that always overtook her when she came up empty.

Since she'd come into the small guest bedroom that doubled as her office over an hour ago, she'd gotten up every few minutes, procrastinating. She'd even dusted the shelves.

Dusted, for pity's sake, something she absolutely abhorred and did only when the dust motes got large enough to put saddles on and ride. She was that desperate to get away from her work.

Nothing was materializing in her brain.

It was time, she decided, to take a temporary reprieve. A real one. Maybe what she needed was to take the morning off. The afternoon had to get better. The only way it would be worse was if she was suddenly possessed to clean out her refrigerator.

Her fingers flying for the first time that day, she pressed a combination of keys and shut her computer down. Things would look different when she opened it up again later, she promised herself.

The house reverberated as the front door was slammed shut. Hurricane Libby, she thought fondly.

"Mama, Mama, come quick!"

Claire smiled to herself. She was accustomed to Libby's "come quick" calls. "Come quick" could mean anything from a call urging her to see a praying mantis, to watching a funny cartoon on television, to seeing a mother bird feeding her babies in the nest they'd discovered out front in their pine tree. Claire had learned very quickly that no matter what pitch the cry was delivered in, it wasn't about anything earthshaking.

Life was very exciting for a four-going-on-five-year-old.

Claire stepped out into the hallway. "What is it this time, Lib?"

Libby, her blond curls bouncing around her head like so many yellow springs in motion, lost no time in finding her. "The man next door needs help."

Claire's brow furrowed. Well, this was definitely a different sort of "come quick" than she was anticipating. He was actually asking for her help? She and the very attractive, very mysterious man next door hadn't even really exchanged any words. She'd said hello a few times, and he had just nodded in response. Not even a "hi." If it weren't for the fact that the mail carrier had delivered a letter to her house intended for him, she wouldn't have even known his name.

Since he'd moved in, she'd seen him only a handful of times, usually on his way to his car early in the morning or returning to the house late in the evening. She never saw him do anything mundane, like mow his grass or take out his garbage. He had a gardener for the former, and as for the latter, Claire doubted that he ate or did very much living at home. Disposal of garbage might be a moot point—he probably didn't have any.

Placing an anchoring hand on Libby's shoulder, Claire held her in place. "What do you mean, 'help'?"

Claire couldn't visualize Mr. Quartermain asking for any, much less asking it of her or using Libby as a messenger. Libby didn't lie, but something wasn't right here.

Impatience hummed through the tiny body. "I asked him, and he said he needs help, lots of it."

Maybe she was being hasty in dismissing Libby's story. "Is anything wrong?"

Slight shoulders lifted and fell in an exaggerated shrug that seemed so natural for the young. "He stole a baby."

Claire's eyes were as huge as Libby's had been. "He did what?"

All innocence, Libby recited, "I think he stole a baby. He said it wasn't his and he needed help with it." With her fingers wrapped firmly around her mother's hand, Libby was already dragging Claire out of the house. "C'mon, Mama, you help better than anyone."

"You're prejudiced, but keep talking. I need the flattery."

Libby liked it when Mama used big words when she talked to her. It meant she was almost all grown up, like Mama. "What's that mean? Pre-joo-dish?"

"Something I'll explain to you when we have more

time." Right now, she had to investigate Libby's story. Claire had to admit, curiosity was getting the better of her. Otherwise, she would have never entertained the thought of just paying Evan Quartermain a "neighborly" visit. Not when he definitely wasn't.

As it turned out, she didn't have to go far to satisfy her curiosity. Evan was still trying to open the front door while wrestling with a car seat and an animated baby sitting in same.

"You're right—he does have a baby." Claire's surprise could have been measured on the Richter scale. Maybe he was divorced, she thought. And his ex-wife unexpectedly had to leave town. That would explain the sudden appearance of the baby, as well as his distraught expression.

"I told you, Mama." Now that she was certain her mother was coming, Libby released Claire's hand and made a dash for Evan's front door.

He had the kind of reflexes that had made his college fencing master proud, but Evan was still having trouble getting his key in the lock without dropping the baby.

"See?" Libby announced proudly, planting herself in front of Evan. "I brought help!"

Evan blew out a breath, then turned to put the baby down on the step, ready to warn Libby to keep her distance.

"I don't—" His words vanished as he found himself looking into the very amused, very bemused eyes of the woman next door.

The chatterbox's mother.

Recognition was a delayed reaction. She didn't exactly look like a mother. Barefoot and in black shorts despite the autumn bite to the weather, the petite blonde looked more like the girl's older sister than her mother. Didn't mothers usually look a little worn, a little frayed around the edges? If anyone had a right to that look, she certainly did, given that she was Libby's mother.

But this woman was *fine,* and the look in her eyes was sheer amusement. At his expense. "Can I help you?" he asked coolly.

He'd all but snapped the words out at her. No doubt about it, the man was not a contender for the Mr. Congeniality award, baby or no baby in his arms. But Claire had to struggle to hold off an attack of the giggles. She doubted if she had ever seen anyone look more uncomfortable than he did. He was holding the baby practically at arm's length, as if he feared any closer contact would make one of them self-destruct.

He didn't like babies very much, she judged. For her part, Claire was a sucker for them, always had been. She loved the scent of them, the feel. She longed to take the baby in her arms, but refrained. No use getting worked up and mushy. After all, it wasn't like it was her baby.

"No," she finally answered, "but I think I can help you."

He almost said *Thank God* out loud as he held out the car seat to her. But she took his keys instead and, with a minimum of fuss, unlocked the door for him.

With a sigh, he entered, still holding the car seat as if he expected the baby to begin throwing up with an eighteen-inch projectile.

When he turned around, he narrowly avoided hitting Claire with the baby seat, but she managed to jump back in time. She nodded at the baby, seeing the resemblance. "I take it that's your daughter?" She ignored Libby tugging urgently on her sweater, knowing a contradiction hovered on the girl's lips.

Evan really didn't feel like discussing his problem with this woman. He wasn't even going to answer, then finally said, "Supposedly."

"'Supposedly'?" she echoed, stunned, taking another look at the fussing child. The baby certainly looked like him, right down to the wave in her hair. Just look at all that hair, she thought, longing to curl her fingers through it. She raised her eyes to Evan. This wasn't making any sense. "Who's the mother?"

Instead of answering, he turned his back on her, setting the baby seat down on the first available flat surface, the top of the two-tier bookcase.

"I don't know." As far as he knew, the child couldn't be his. He'd always used precautions.

It took very little imagination on Claire's part for her to see the baby seat plummeting from its perch. Was he crazy? She picked it up and thrust it back into his hands.

"If you're not careful, she'll fall off. And what do you mean, you don't know?" How did he get this baby, then?

"Just what I said." Evan stared at her, surprised, as his arms were suddenly filled with baby again. He saw where Libby got her pushiness from. "She was just left, on my doorstep, so to speak—actually, on my secretary's desk at the office."

He looked at his watch again. Damn it, time was growing short. Desperate—that was the only word to describe his mood—he decided to take a chance. "Look, are you any good with kids?"

Claire ran her hand along the waves and curls of her daughter's hair, hair that was no mean feat to comb in the morning. "I haven't broken the one I have."

If that was a joke, he didn't have time for humor. "Great. How would you like to earn some extra money?"

She frowned. Normally, she'd tell him what he could do with his money. Spend it on his "supposed" daughter. But this past month had been rough, and Claire was in no position to turn down work that fell into her lap. Any reasonable work, she amended for her own sake.

"Just what did you have in mind?"

Chapter Two

There was amusement in her eyes. He didn't have the luxury of being able to take offense. Right now, he needed to prevail upon the good graces of a woman he hardly knew, even by sight.

"What I have in mind," he began, rewording her question, "is someone to take care of, um..." He was drawing a blank.

Stunned, Evan searched his mind and realized that, for the life of him, he couldn't remember the baby's name.

The woman's amused expression was intensifying. Muttering under his breath, he shifted baby and seat over onto his hip and he dug into his pocket. Evan had taken the note he'd found pinned to the baby's shirt with him to scrutinize later and perhaps somehow identify whoever was responsible for this dilemma he found himself in.

Pulling it out now, he looked down, scanning it. "Rachel."

He looked up at Claire with a mixture of hope and expectation, waiting for her to agree.

Libby was at his side, peering at the note in his hand. Mama had taught her how to read a few words, but everything on that paper looked like scribbles to her.

"You have to write down your baby's name? Don't you know it?" Libby's face puckered as she tried to puzzle out his behavior. "Everybody knows their baby's name," she stated with the confidence of the very young. "How come you have to write it down?" Compassion, learned at her mother's knee, filled her expressive eyes as she continued looking up at him. "Doesn't your remembery work?"

Claire affectionately passed her hand over the curls. "Memory," she corrected.

"Memory," Libby repeated, nodding in agreement. She didn't mind being corrected. Mama had told her that was the way she learned, and she loved to learn.

He felt as if he was being ganged up on by a gang comprised of one and two-thirds women, if he counted Rachel in on it.

"My memory works just fine, and she's not my baby," Evan snapped. He didn't know who needed more convincing of that, his neighbor, Libby or him.

Ingrained instincts had Claire's hand tightening on Libby's shoulder, moving the girl behind her in an age-old gesture of protectiveness.

"You don't have to shout," Claire admonished him, raising her own voice.

Why was she pushing her daughter behind her? Did the woman think he was going to strike her? Where the hell did she get that idea? He was just frustrated, but he wasn't a monster.

"I am not shouting." And then, because he was, Evan lowered his voice, struggling with exasperation. "I am not shouting," he repeated. "It's just been a very trying morning."

She heard the weary note in his voice and saw the confusion in his eyes that he was trying to hide. Normally given to sympathy, Claire relented. He wasn't as certain that he had no hand in fathering this baby as he was claiming, she thought.

"I can see that," she said quietly.

Something within him reached out to the sympathy in her voice before he could think better of it. He didn't need sympathy; he needed a baby-sitter.

"You know, I don't even know your name," he realized out loud.

"I'm not surprised." After all, he'd made no attempt to talk to her the few times their paths had crossed. Quite the opposite, actually. Whenever she did see him, he'd hurried away, as if exchanging any sort of pleasantries was superfluous behavior.

"Mama's name is Claire," Libby announced. "She's got another name, and it's like mine. Walker. What's your other name?" Libby had asked the man his name before, but he'd never told her. She thought now was a good time to find out, since they were talking about names.

Claire. It made him think of someone old-fashioned. Someone quiet. So much for a perfect match. "Quartermain," he told Libby, but his eyes were on Claire. "Evan Quartermain."

A smile, still amused, but softer somehow, he thought, graced her mouth.

"How do you do, Evan Quartermain?"

"Lousy," he answered honestly. Apparently unable to find satisfaction by trying to eat her foot, Rachel began to fuss again. He really didn't have time for this. Evan held out his burden toward Claire. "So, Claire, will you?"

He still hadn't made the terms clear, and she knew the danger of agreements made without boundaries. "Will I what?"

Was she being obtuse on purpose? "Will you take care

of the baby? Rachel," he amended. Then, when she gave no answer, he said, "Her!" For emphasis, Evan thrust the baby seat even farther toward Claire.

Because she felt sorry for Rachel and because she was afraid of where Evan might decide to swing the seat next, Claire grabbed hold of the sides and took it from him.

"You're going to make her sick," she chided with a sternness she used on Libby only when the girl was particularly trying.

Both her tone and her expression softened as she looked down at the small, puckered face that was about to let out another lusty yell. She angled the seat so that Libby could get a good view, as well.

Claire ran the side of her finger along the silky, damp cheek. "It's okay, honey, I've got you now. No more wild rides with Mr. Grump."

Claire raised her eyes to his. The soft expression faded slowly, like sunlight descending into shadows. He couldn't tell exactly what she thought of him and he really didn't care—as long as she helped him out.

Something told Claire she was going to regret this, but she couldn't bring herself to just turn her back on the baby. She knew others who could, but that wasn't her way. Claire pressed her lips together, prepared to make the best of this.

"How long a time are we talking about? An hour? Two?"

He could lie to her, Evan supposed. But he hated lies. For one thing, the truth was difficult enough to keep track of. Lies were impossible, even little ones.

"For openers," he began, watching her face, "the rest of the afternoon."

Openers? And what exactly did that mean? She had a strange feeling that she didn't want to know. What had started out as a neighborly response to a cry for help was quickly turning into something else. She was beginning to feel like an innocent insect that had flown unknowingly into a spider web.

But one look at Rachel's face told her that struggling was useless. Still, she couldn't let him know that. He seemed the type to take advantage.

Claire began to shake her head. "I don't—"

He wouldn't lie, but he was not above bribery in matters that counted. And he was desperate. Without thinking, he placed his hands on her arms in supplication, framing her body.

"Look, I was serious when I said I'd pay you. I will, really. Any amount, I just—" He was babbling like a fool, he upbraided himself. Evan took another deep breath, making a heartfelt appeal to, he hoped, her better instincts. "I'm just really in a bind."

The idea of fatherhood really had him baffled, she thought. Claire glanced at Rachel before looking back at Evan. Just what was the story behind the gentleman and the baby? Rachel obviously looked as if she was his daughter. They had the same black hair, the same green eyes. Most babies' eyes were blue when they were this young. To have a distinct color so early really pointed a finger at her parentage.

"I can see that."

Relief began to surface in Evan, only to founder when she added, "And your sense of smell isn't too keen, either."

Eyebrows narrowed over a nose that sculptors only prayed they could duplicate. "Sense of smell?"

She didn't think she was talking in code. He was so hopelessly out of his league right now, it was as if all his faculties had been anesthetized.

With a quick nod for his benefit, Claire indicated Rachel. "Your daughter's ripe, Mr. Quartermain. I'd say she needed changing about fifteen minutes ago." He should have attended to that immediately. That he didn't just underscored how hopelessly inexperienced he was.

"Changing?" Evan looked around as if he expected a diaper to materialize out of thin air. Well, why the hell not? Rachel had. When his eyes returned to Claire's face, they were tinged with disbelief. She couldn't possibly mean that she thought *he* should do the changing. He hadn't the faintest idea where to begin.

This was one dyed-in-the-wool bachelor, Claire thought. Pity filled her—not for Evan, but for the baby.

"Come with me," she instructed. Still carrying the baby seat, Claire walked to the front door. The lack of movement behind her told her that he wasn't following. She looked over her shoulder at Evan expectantly. "Well?"

This was a dream, he thought, a bad dream. Any second, he was going to wake up and find that he'd just fallen asleep over the report he'd been reading. It certainly had been boring enough to put him out.

But he didn't wake up. This was miserably real.

Ten small fingers were wrapping themselves around his hand like miniature tentacles of an octopus. Libby pulled at him. "Mama says to come."

What was he, a dog?

Grudgingly, Evan followed in Claire's wake, noting, purely on a disinterested level, that her wake was quite an attractive one.

"I think I still have a box of Libby's old diapers," Claire was saying to him as she walked into her own living room.

Still holding on to his hand, Libby pouted. "I don't wear diapers, Mama."

She'd embarrassed her, Claire thought, and delicately retraced her verbal steps. "Not anymore, but you did when you were Rachel's age. Everybody did, honey." She glanced at Evan. "Even Mr. Quartermain."

The thought of the tall, serious-looking man beside her

wearing diapers had Libby releasing his hand to cover her mouth as giggles pealed out. She nearly fell on the floor, laughing.

Satisfied, Claire set the baby seat down on the coffee table. Wide and square, it looked as if it were built to support an elephant.

"Actually, I never used the ones I'm going to lend you," she told Evan. "They're cloth diapers someone gave me at my shower. Disposable ones were the only kind I had time for back then." She grinned, looking at her daughter. "You were quite a handful when you were a baby."

In Evan's opinion, her "handful" had only intensified with time.

"Why don't you watch your—Rachel," Claire amended for the sake of argument, "while I go see if I can dig up the box in the garage?"

He had to get going. "But I—" he began futilely, addressing the words to her back.

Evan didn't get an opportunity to finish his protest before she disappeared. A snowball in hell had more of a chance of remaining intact than he had of finishing a sentence around these two, he thought grudgingly. Not that the woman would listen to anything he had to say, even if he had managed to complete it. Claire Walker had a mind all her own, just as her daughter did.

He didn't know which one he found more annoying.

Evan wrinkled his nose as the air seemed to shift. She'd been right about Rachel being ripe. Wow.

He looked down at the baby in complete awe. How could anything so…? Well, all right, he supposed she was cute if you liked babies, but how could anything that looked so cute smell so bad?

As if in response to the silent criticism, Rachel began to cry. Really cry.

She looked as if she was in pain, he thought. Panic and

frustration tore at him in equal portions. Now what did he do?

He was aware of a tugging on his arm. Libby again.

"Want me to hold her?" she asked brightly. "I'm real good at holding things. Even the cat when she wriggles." Libby was fully prepared to give him an immediate demonstration.

"No, I don't want you holding her." For all of Libby's energy, she didn't look all that much bigger than the baby did. It didn't take much imagination on his part to envision her dropping Rachel.

And then the rest of her statement registered. "You have a cat?"

He looked around for telltale signs. A scratching post, or, in lieu of that, scratched-up furniture. Cats always made him sneeze violently, yet there wasn't even a tickle. Maybe there really was something wrong with his nose, he thought.

Libby's wide smile drooped instantly. "We did. But she ran away." Her sigh was so deep, Evan had the impression that she had let all the air out of her body. "Mama says sometimes things you love do that. They just go away." Suddenly hopeful, she asked, "You haven't seen her, have you? She's white and pretty and really soft."

"No, I haven't seen her." Although, at the moment he wished there *was* a cat around—getting a stuffed-up nose might be a good thing. Rachel's aroma seemed to be deepening. "Go see what's keeping your mother."

But Libby stayed where she was, cocking her head as she looked up at him. He talked funny. "Nothing's keeping her, silly. She's free."

"I mean—" Evan sighed, giving up. He had absolutely no idea how to talk to someone who came up to his belt buckle.

He would have to find Claire himself. For a moment, he debated leaving Rachel where she was and instructing Libby to watch her. After all, Rachel wasn't about to execute a half gainer off the table. But Libby might. There was nothing to do but take the baby with him.

What the hell had he ever done to deserve this?

As he picked up the seat again, Rachel ceased fussing and stared at him with what looked like wonder in her eyes. Opened so wide, they looked as if they took up half her face. Her expression reminded him of one of his sisters. She looked like Paige, he realized suddenly, then dismissed the thought. All babies tended to look alike. It didn't mean anything.

The burden in his arms began to feel progressively heavier to him as he walked in the general direction Claire had taken. She'd said something about the garage.

Pausing, he asked Libby, "Where's your garage?"

Libby's tolerant smile was reminiscent of her mother's. "Outside."

Strength, he needed strength. "I mean, how do I get to it from inside your house? Where did your mother go?" He enunciated each word slowly, clearly and sharply while trying not to lose his temper.

"I'm right here," Claire announced, returning. "Did you miss me?" she couldn't resist asking.

Evan looked like the poster child for the beleaguered and the befuddled. Not to mention the angry. She imagined that the latter emotion was directed at the world in general and probably at her specifically. His type always had to have someone to blame, which was a pity, she thought, because he was kind of cute.

Evan turned around at the sound of her voice. "Can you take her now?" It came out less of a question than a demand.

"Not yet," she answered patiently. "My hands are full."

"What is all that?" he asked. She had a blanket slung over her shoulder and a box tucked under her arm, and she was dragging something along that looked like netting strung over tubes.

"Your salvation," she said glibly.

While searching for the box of cloth diapers she'd packed away, Claire had come across the Portacrib. She'd decided that it wouldn't be a bad idea to bring it out, as well. After all, the baby was going to need someplace to sleep, and she knew without asking that Evan didn't have anything. She could lend him a few things. Any furniture that Libby hadn't managed to destroy in her exuberance, Claire had saved in hopes that someday another, possibly more quiet baby would make use of it. She wanted more children than just one. One, she had grown up feeling, was a very lonely number.

Claire leaned the collapsed crib against the side of the sofa. "I guess since time is of the essence for you, we'll set up here for now."

Depositing the box of diapers on the coffee table, Claire spread out the blanket on the sofa. "All right, I think we're all ready."

"Great." He set down the baby seat on the table beside the box and lost no time in initiating his retreat.

Only to be stopped in his tracks.

"Not so fast, Evan."

Now what did she want? "But I—"

"—need a demonstration." She wasn't about to let him fast-talk his way out of this.

Evan stared at her. Communication between them had just ground to a standstill. "Of what?"

He was either very dense or very stubborn. Or both. She opted for the last choice. "Of how to change the baby."

What made her think he wanted a demonstration? "I don't have time for this."

If he wanted to play it that way, so could she. "All right,

then I don't have time to watch her.'' Picking up the seat, she presented it to Evan. "Sorry. Those are my terms.''

Maybe it was the smell, but his brain was definitely in a fog. He had no idea what she was talking about. "What are your terms?''

Claire grinned. She heard surrender in his voice. In the face of that, she could afford to be magnanimous.

"I'm making them up as I go along." Setting the seat down again, she undid the straps restraining Rachel, then lifted her out. Gingerly, Claire tucked her arm around the baby, who was soaked. "But I really want you to try your hand at changing the baby.''

He remained rooted to the spot. There was no way he was about to touch that. "Into what?''

Claire gave him a look. "Into dry diapers.''

"You mean open up that—?'' There was horror written all over his face. He'd sooner put up with a first-class, intensified audit than attempt to remove Rachel's very heavy diaper.

Libby erupted into a fit of giggles, not bothering to cover her mouth this time. The sound was infectious, and Claire found it difficult not to join in. And impossible to keep the smile from her lips.

Gently, she laid Rachel down in the center of the blanket and slipped off the soggy pajama bottoms. "That is *exactly* what I mean. You obviously don't know how, and there's no time like the present to learn.''

Was she out of her mind? "Why would I want to learn?''

Claire dropped the pajama bottoms in a little heap on the blanket and looked at him. She answered patiently, speaking to him as if she were trying to make a child understand something that was just beyond his reach.

"I have a little news flash for you—the number of times you change a baby is disproportionate to its size." She considered that for a moment. Math had never been her strong suit. "Or maybe the inverse. At any rate, the smaller they are, the more they need to be changed. And at this stage of her life, Rachel is going to need a lot of changing."

All right, he understood that part of it. But why did he have to learn how to do it? "But you're going to be—"

"Helping out," Claire supplied, and squashed any other belief he had been entertaining. "I don't intend to be her permanent nanny. I have a business to run."

"A business?" Evan echoed in disbelief. "You?"

It was a rare thing for Claire to get angry. She liked to think of herself as a reasonable and even-tempered woman. But she knew an insult when one was hovering in front of her.

"You say that as if you don't believe that's possible. Why?"

As if in reply, Evan glanced down at her long legs curled beneath her as she sat on the edge of the sofa, and at her clothes, which lovingly adhered to her body. Businesswoman wouldn't have been the first label he would have pinned to her. Nor the second. She looked as if she would be more at home on the cover of a magazine than undertaking any sort of business venture.

But this wasn't the time to get into that. "No reason." And then he looked at his watch again. This was taking far longer than he had anticipated. He still had to go over his notes before he went into the meeting. "Look, I'm really pressed for time."

"You keep saying that." And it was obvious from her expression that she neither believed his protest nor was going to accept it. "Make time. She obviously must mean something to you or you wouldn't have her."

The leap from point A to point B seemed to have been made entirely without reason. Evan's brow furrowed as he tried to make sense of it and failed. "What kind of logic is that?"

"Mine," she informed him blithely. "Now, then, shall we?" Claire patted the blanket in an open invitation.

Not to be left out of the project, Libby demanded, "What can I do? What can I do?"

Wedging in between Evan and the baby on the sofa, Libby pranced from foot to foot as if the ground were too hot for her to stand on in any one place for more than a second.

Evan assumed that Claire would tell her daughter to stand aside and be quiet—that's what he would have done. But Claire didn't do what was expected. He had a feeling the statement covered a lot of territory.

"Get me some tissues, Lib. I don't have any wipes," she explained to Evan as if he even knew what those were. "So tissues are going to have to do in a pinch. And a washcloth," she called out to her daughter. "Run some warm water over it, honey. And be sure to wring it out."

Claire emphasized the last part, knowing if she didn't, Libby was going to leave a trail of water all the way from the bathroom sink to the sofa.

Waiting, Claire cooed soft words at the baby that Evan could only half make out. But the tone was soothing. And it worked, he noticed. Rachel was calming down. Maybe this would work out after all, at least for now.

Claire stripped Rachel down to her diaper, then leaned back and gestured for Evan to take over. "All right, go ahead."

Evan felt something sicken in his stomach. "Go ahead?" he repeated dumbly.

Why was he acting as if his brain level had suddenly been reduced to that of a potato?

"Change her," Claire urged, moving aside for him to have clear access. "The grand opening awaits."

He actually reached out one hand before he stopped. He

just couldn't go through with this, not for any amount of money in the world.

"I don't— I've never—" He looked at her helplessly, falling back on the only thing he'd learned that worked. "How much do you want per diaper?"

"That's pathetic," she informed him. Then, with a tolerant sigh, Claire elbowed him out of the way. Evan was never so glad to move aside in his life. "Watch and learn," she instructed, taking her place again.

Rachel began to kick, churning up the mess within, he guessed.

"Libby?" Claire called out expectantly.

The streak wearing pink overalls zipped back to her side, with a box of tissues in one hand and a slightly dripping washcloth in the other. "Here, Mama."

Claire took them as solemnly as if she were receiving a knight's sword and shield. She set both items on the table.

Evan forced himself to watch. He got as far as seeing Claire tear off the tabs on either side of the kicking chubby legs before he averted his eyes.

"Yuck!" Libby pronounced.

For once, Evan thought, the little girl was guilty of understatement.

Chapter Three

The first thing Evan did when he returned to his office was call Devin. Maybe it wasn't an entirely rational decision on his part, given that Devin was four hundred miles away. But Evan knew that if anyone could find out who the mother of this child was, it was Devin. His brother had a knack for locating missing people. Distance wouldn't be a problem.

Why Devin wanted to spend his life in pursuit of people who, for all intents and purposes, had vanished was beyond Evan's comprehension. In his opinion, finding them didn't pay nearly enough to compensate for the effort involved. But for the first time in his life, Evan was actually glad his brother had decided to become a private investigator.

As soon as he heard the receiver being picked up on the other end, Evan asked, "Are you busy?"

There was a pause, and for a second, Evan was afraid that he'd gotten Devin's answering machine. He was in no mood to deal with recorded messages and was about to hang up when he heard, "Depends on who's asking. If it's the IRS, the answer is no. If it's the competition trying to see how I'm doing, then the answer is yes. Truth is located somewhere in between.''

Evan didn't need to see his face to know that Devin was grinning. They hadn't shared the same sense of humor since a year after puberty had hit.

''It's me, Devin. Evan,'' he added impatiently when there was no response on the other end.

The deep chuckle told Evan that his brother had known all along who was calling. ''And a hello to you, too, brother,'' Devin replied. ''Don't you believe in preliminary niceties anymore?''

''You're the last one to give a lecture about that.'' Evan had always been the one who lived by the rules, who crossed every *t* and dotted every *i*. That was why this turn of events seemed so incredible, so unfair if it was true. He'd always taken precautions, for heaven's sake.

Except, he realized suddenly, that one time.

The fruity taste of the Mai-tais had hidden their potent punch, and he'd downed one after another until he'd found himself acting amorous and passionate—entirely out of character.

No, he refused to believe that that one night, which was mostly a blur anyway, could have resulted in the fifteen-pound bundle he'd had delivered to his office.

''Look,'' Evan said sharply, ''I didn't call to argue about protocol.''

Accustomed to his brother's abrupt manner, Devin was unfazed by the annoyed tone. ''Nice to know. Why did you call?''

Evan was aware that he was gripping the receiver too tightly. He hated asking Devin for a favor, even one he was planning on paying for. ''I need you to find someone for me.''

If Devin was surprised by the request, he hid it well. "All right, what's the person's name?"

Evan thought of the note. There'd been no signature on it. "I don't know."

That made it harder, but not impossible. Half of the people Devin had looked for were nameless to him when he began his search. "Description?"

Irritation, fueled by frustration, began to mount. Evan knew he sounded like a fool. He could just visualize Devin smirking at him. "I don't have one. That is, I do, a few, but none of them might be the right one."

If Devin was smirking, he gave no indication of it. Instead, he sounded concerned. "Evan, you okay? You sound...addled."

It wasn't a word that Devin would have used to describe his brother under normal circumstances. Yet addled was exactly how Evan sounded—as if something had just happened to shake him up. This had to be big. Evan didn't rattle easily—at least, not enough to come to his brother for help.

Evan bristled. He didn't care for the observation, however deserving it might be. "You'd be addled, too, if someone just left a baby in your office and said it was yours."

Devin let out a low whistle. "Someone left you a baby?"

Had his brother suddenly gone deaf? "I just said that," Evan snapped.

Devin wasn't slow, but when it came to his work, he believed in being methodical. That meant getting all the facts down straight the first time around. "And it's not yours."

"No." The denial was quick, decisive. And untrue. "That is, I don't think so." Evan's wavering deteriorated even further. "I don't know."

Right now, it didn't strike Devin that his brother knew

a hell of a whole lot, but this wasn't the time to point that little tidbit out.

"And the person you want me to find is...?" His sentence trailed off as he waited for Evan to complete it for him.

Was Devin playing games at his expense? "The baby's mother, naturally."

Devin blocked out his brother's tone. Letting it get under his skin wasn't going to do either of them any good.

"Do you have any idea who she might be, Evan? Anything at all for me to go on?"

Yes, he had something for Devin to go on. Something he didn't want to admit to. His night of the endless Maitai. Evan ran a hand through his hair, bracing himself. If Devin was going to be of any use, he had to tell his brother everything.

"My best guess is that it might be this entertainer I met on a cruise ship. A singer," he added. If he'd been sober, this would never have happened. He wouldn't have thought of flirting with a woman he didn't know, much less bedding her.

Or had she flirted with him? Evan tried hard to remember, but it was all one heated blur with very little of it clear.

"Why, Evan, you sly devil. And here I thought you were married to your work." His laughter obliterated anything else Devin might have said for more than a minute. "Boy, did I ever have you pegged wrong."

Evan didn't care for being the source of Devin's amusement. If he could have, he would have slammed the phone down in his brother's ear. But now wasn't the time to take offense.

He needed Devin. But he also needed his privacy, and a thought had suddenly occurred to him. "Look, not a word of this to the girls and Mother, do you hear?"

"Raise your voice any louder, and everyone between

Newport Beach and San Francisco will hear.'' Devin paused, as if considering something. ''Send me a dollar.''

Evan thought he must have heard wrong. Devin was making even less sense than he normally did. And if this was a joke, it wasn't funny. ''What?''

''Send me a dollar,'' Devin repeated mildly. ''Then you'll be a client and I won't be able to tell them anything, even if they try to wheedle the information out of me.''

Evan knew his sisters were more than capable of getting a stone to talk if they set their minds to it. Determination, in one form or another, was a strain that ran through them all.

''You find out who this is, and I'll send you more than a dollar. I intend to pay you for your services, you know,'' he added, feeling somewhat uncomfortable about the whole arrangement. He didn't want Devin getting the wrong impression. ''I'm not asking for charity.''

Nothing changed. Evan was as uptight as ever. Devin blew out a breath. ''In case you haven't looked in the mirror lately, Evan, we're brothers. It's not called charity when it's between family.''

Still, if you paid for something, you got what you paid for. ''I'd feel better paying you.''

''Well, I wouldn't.'' There was a note of annoyance in his voice. There were lessons Evan had never learned, he thought. He wondered if his brother ever would. But now wasn't the time for that, either. Devin got down to business. ''How old is this baby?''

''You know I'm not any good at things like that.'' But because Devin obviously wanted an answer, Evan thought for a minute, remembering the note. It had mentioned taking care of the baby for six months. ''About six months old or so.''

Devin did a quick calculation. ''I'm going to need a list

of the names, numbers and addresses of the women you've been intimate with within the last two years or so.''

The laugh that met the request was dry and without humor. "Won't be much of a list." He waited for Devin to make some sort of snide comment. But Evan was disappointed.

"Good, I won't have that much work to do. I'm really busy with another case, as it is.''

So Devin was working. No ego, no attempt at crowing or rubbing the matter in. Maybe he'd been too hard on Devin, after all. Evan thought a minute. "How about the cruise entertainer?''

She was the first one Devin intended to question. "By all means, include her.''

It wasn't that easy. "I haven't got an address for her, or a number. Or a name, for that matter,'' he added, thinking out loud. "She called herself Siren.''

"Original,'' Devin commented dryly. "That's where the detecting part comes in, brother of mine.'' He tapped a pencil on his desk, thinking. "I'll need the name of the cruise line—and anything else you can think of. Fax everything to me when you're ready.''

Evan was ready now. "I don't have to fax it—I can give you everything you asked for right now.''

Jotting them down for his own sake as he went, Evan recited the women's names. There was a grand total of three. He added in everything that seemed relevant, including the fact that as far as he knew, two of them were in relationships now. They might even be married. He'd lost touch.

"You're right,'' Devin agreed, looking the names over. "It's a short list. Sure you haven't forgotten anyone?''

Evan knew that Devin hadn't meant it as a criticism, but it still smarted. "You're the one who's always had women pounding at your door, not me.''

His brother was referring to their formative years, Devin thought with a smile, when for some damn reason, Evan had hung back, refusing to avail himself of the ready companionship that was out there. But that was all in the past. These days, Devin had more-serious thoughts on his mind than the easy, pleasurable loving of willing women. More and more, one woman was beginning to take center stage.

"Only because you weren't interested," Devin reminded him. He had the feeling his brother could do with someone in his corner. "Look, like I said, I'm busy with another case right now, but I can take a commuter flight and be up there in forty-five minutes if you need me."

The offer was unexpected and appreciated, even if Evan didn't know exactly how to make that fact known without embarrassing both himself and his brother. Because he didn't know how else to do it, he let it slide without comment.

"Just find whoever's responsible for this charade. Oh, there's a note." He suddenly realized he hadn't mentioned that. "Doesn't say very much, but maybe you can match the handwriting to a signature on the DMV applications."

Devin smiled to himself. Evan was giving him a hell of a lot of credit. "You must think I can work magic."

For the first time, Evan allowed himself a hint of a smile. Maybe it was going to be all right, after all. "No, just that you're underhanded."

"You certainly know how to flatter a guy. Fax the note," he told Evan. "I'll do what I can. Call you later," he promised.

"Thanks." Evan couldn't say more than that. It was enough.

Evan broke off the connection and then quickly redialed his brother's number while feeding the wrinkled note into his fax machine.

The note was just slipping out the other end when Alma

knocked and opened the door. She appeared surprised to see Evan faxing. She usually took care of that sort of thing for him.

"Yes?" Like a man with something to hide, he quickly slipped the note back into his pocket.

Curious, she managed not to show it. Alma was the soul of business. "Mr. Donovan and the gentlemen from Japan are waiting for you in the conference room." She could see he'd forgotten.

Damn, and he hadn't reviewed the notes yet. Maybe he should have handled that first, Evan upbraided himself. Now he was going to have to fly by the seat of his pants, and this wasn't the time for maiden runs.

It wasn't a very comforting thought. He wasn't the spontaneous type. But it looked as if he was going to have to learn. Adam Donovan wasn't a man to be kept waiting, especially by a man he had taken under his wing.

"Tell them I'll be right there," Evan promised without looking in her direction. He gathered up the folder with his notes and charts and hoped he hadn't forgotten anything.

This little ordeal with the baby couldn't have happened at a more inopportune time.

But then, Evan thought as he walked out of the office, he doubted that there could have ever been an opportune time for this to occur.

He just hoped Devin could come through with something.

The slow boil that had been going on all evening now reached critical mass and threatened to scald everything in its path.

Claire was angry, really angry. There was absolutely no excuse for this. She had agreed to take care of Evan Quartermain's daughter—or alleged daughter, as he probably thought of her—not because of him, but because she felt sorry for Rachel. It was obvious that the man was more concerned about getting back to his office than he was about the little girl's welfare. Claire was surprised, now that she thought of it, that Evan hadn't just left the baby sitting in her infant seat in front of the television set until he returned.

Which he hadn't done.

But, she continued with her mental tirade, she'd agreed to watch Rachel for a few hours, not a few days.

Claire stared out the window that faced the street, just as she had done on a fairly regular basis since she had put Libby to bed three hours ago. Libby had resisted bedtime with even more vigor than usual. Once in bed, she'd popped up four times like overdone toast, getting up on one pretext or another and returning to the living room where Claire had set up the Portacrib. Libby just couldn't get enough of the baby.

Unlike Evan Quartermain.

Though she could see perfectly well through the opaque white curtains, Claire pushed them back.

No telltale beam of headlights approaching from a distance. No sound of a car.

Nothing.

The residential street where they both lived lay wrapped in soft slumber.

Where the hell was he? And just who did he think he was, staying out until all hours while she tended to his baby?

His baby, not hers. His.

And there was no doubt in her mind that it was his. Rachel even smiled like Evan did. She looked as if there was a gas bubble building in the middle of her chest. The same could be said about his smile—it was small and offered under duress.

The tiny wail finally penetrated her consciousness, interrupting her silent railings against the missing Quartermain. She crossed quickly to Rachel before her cries could carry to Libby's room.

That was all she needed, Claire thought, to have Libby out here again, offering to help. Libby was already completely enamored with Rachel, treating her like a cross between a little sister and a new, anatomically correct doll.

"Hush, I'm here, I'm here," she murmured in a voice that sounded far more soothing and subdued than she actually felt.

Claire lifted the small bundle into her arms, automatically feeling Rachel's bottom. Dry, thank goodness. She'd already gone through all the diapers she'd found. By four o'clock, she'd had to make a quick run to the store, both children in tow, to buy disposable ones, as well as more milk. For every ounce she took in, Rachel produced four.

"You're about six months old, I'd guess. Haven't you learned how to sleep through the night yet?" she asked. Rachel's reply was to wail louder. Rocking her, Claire rubbed concentric circles along the baby's back. "I thought Libby was the only one who refused to learn."

At almost five years old, Libby still insisted on waking up three or four times a night and calling for her each time. Claire was unable to turn a deaf ear no matter what her pediatrician advised; there was a rut worn in the rug between her room and her daughter's.

"If it were me, I'd love to have someone fuss over me and then put me to bed. I'd go out just like that." She snapped her fingers, catching Rachel's attention. The sobs softened, then disappeared. "Okay, one more song and then it's over between us, you hear?" she warned Rachel.

Rachel responded by making a noise and then sucking on Claire's shoulder. Claire laughed softly, extracting the material from the baby's mouth.

"You're just trying to soften me up, that's all. Well,

don't think I'm a pushover just because I pick you up every time you cry. I'm not. I have no intentions of letting you get to me. I've got a daughter of my own, and that's quite enough, thank you very much. This is just a one-night stand between us. Understood?''

A one-night stand was most likely exactly what had taken place between Rachel's mother and the man who was supposed to have been here hours ago, Claire thought darkly.

He probably thought he could just enjoy himself without any consequences, then balked when consequences insisted on occurring.

The miserable, self-centered…

No, that wasn't fair of her, Claire chided silently. It wasn't fair to condemn Evan Quartermain just because Jack had walked out on her as soon as she had told him she was pregnant. Not everyone was like Jack.

Her mouth quirked into a hollow smile as she paced about the perimeter of the room.

Funny how quickly undying love could die in the face of a tiny stick turning blue.

Rachel seemed to be burrowing against her shoulder. If she didn't know any better, Claire would have said the little girl was almost cuddling. Claire fought hard not to give in to the warm feeling threatening to engulf her. She had no intentions of getting attached to this baby. She'd already learned the dangers of forming attachments to things that were only passing through her life. Rachel would be in and out in a blink of an eye. Once Evan finally showed up.

Claire forced herself to concentrate on her anger. It wasn't difficult. She'd already called his house several times, in case he'd somehow slipped in without her noticing. But there was only his answering machine to listen to her. Calling his office had yielded the same result, except that there she was talking to his voice mail.

You'd think that with all these messages being left, one of them would get through, she thought angrily.

Rachel began to cry again.

"Tell me about it," Claire muttered. "I know, I know, I promised you a song. Okay, here goes."

Maybe singing would take both their minds off the fact that Evan wasn't here.

When morning came and Evan didn't, it was the last straw.

Trying very hard to bridle her anger, Claire hustled Libby into clothes, took along some of Libby's outgrown things to use as a change of clothing for Rachel and bundled them both into her car.

If Muhammad refused to return to the mountain, the damn mountain was going to go to his office looking for him, she thought hotly.

Claire took a deep breath before she turned the key in the ignition. She couldn't afford to drive feeling as angry as she did. Unless, of course, Evan Quartermain were standing in front of the car.

Sitting in the back seat beside the baby's car seat, Libby was the soul of excitement and hope.

"Does this mean we're going to keep Rachel?" Only the seat belt kept her from jumping up and down in her glee. "He didn't come back for her," she explained needlessly.

Claire schooled herself not to say anything in front of Libby that she'd regret, or worse, that Libby would instantly absorb as her phrase of the week.

"Yes, I know that and no, we are not keeping Rachel. Right now, we're doing fine, just the two of us, understand?" Libby nodded, but Claire knew that she wasn't happy about it.

"Then why are we going out again?" Libby wanted to know. "Are we out of diapers again?"

"No, we're not, but that's not because Rachel hasn't been trying." Claire was grateful that the brunt of morning traffic had passed. She wasn't in the mood to be stuck on the road behind some truck with two live wires in the car. "We're going to Mr. Quartermain's office to remind him that he forgot something at our house last night."

He hadn't come over and, as far as she knew, he hadn't even come home. She'd remained awake until midnight, and then Rachel had woken her up at two and then again at six. There'd been no signs of anyone being at home next door any of those times.

This morning, sick of his answering machine, Claire had gone over and banged on his door, to no avail. That was when she'd decided that he probably hadn't returned home at all. His newspaper was still lying out front in his driveway.

By now, he'd been demoted to a life-form that was barely just ahead of the cockroach. And she was beginning to think that she was insulting the roaches.

Libby wasn't about to give up easily. There was too much of Claire in her. "But if he doesn't want her, we can keep her, then, right, Mama?"

"Wrong, Libby. She's a baby, she's not a wallet we found in the street. We can't take her to lost and found and hope nobody claims her."

Libby wasn't quite sure she understood all that, but she nodded anyway. "I know that."

Claire spared her a smile. It wasn't Libby's fault she had a big heart. She came by it honestly. "Then you should know that we can't keep people."

Her eyes were still hopeful. "But we can adopt them, right?"

Adopt. The word stung. Claire sighed, annoyed with herself. Was she ever going to hear that word without a pang?

Claire banked down her feelings. She had more-important things to think about now.

"Wrong, sweetie. And where did you hear about that, anyway?" They hadn't talked about adoption. There was no reason to. It wasn't as if Libby was adopted, the way Claire had been. A little fact her father had failed to tell her until he was on his deathbed. The revelation had completely shaken her up, but she'd learned to deal with it and go on.

"On TV," Libby informed her brightly.

She might have known. Libby retained absolutely everything she came in contact with—like flypaper. Maybe she should start monitoring those children's programs, Claire thought.

She pulled up against the building in a space marked Guest Parking. She didn't feel like a guest. She felt like a very angry woman whose good nature had been taken advantage of.

"Okay, we're here," she announced to her crew.

With Rachel nestled against her shoulder and one hand restraining Libby—who looked poised to run off in several directions at once—Claire rode up the seven flights to Evan's office. She was eternally grateful she'd had the presence of mind to ask him for his business card before he'd left her house yesterday.

Her hand in Libby's, she marched down the hall like an avenging fury. She would have marched straight into his office if not for the woman whose desk was in the outer office.

Gaping at the two children, Alma was on her feet instantly, blocking Evan's door. "You can't go in there."

Claire wasn't about to be put off by any of Evan Quartermain's minions. Her eyes narrowed as she fixed Alma with a look guaranteed to burn holes in wood.

"I wouldn't try to stop me if I were you. I'm here to see

Evan Quartermain and I'm here to see him now." She indicated the baby in her arms. "This is his problem, not mine."

Alma was barely one step ahead of the woman as she flung her small body into Evan's office. "Mr. Quartermain, they're multiplying like rabbits."

Evan looked up. His head hurt. He felt as if there was more information in it now than in the data base of his computer. Yesterday's meeting had broken for dinner, then gone on into the small hours of the morning. They were attempting to forestall a hostile takeover they had gotten wind of, and there had been no time for him to go home. Evan had spent the night on the sofa and showered in the penthouse washroom. He still felt as if he had been summarily chewed up and spit out, and he was in no mood for riddles.

"What are you talking about?"

"Babies," she declared in a voice that might have been used by one of the ancient Egyptians when they had spoken of descending locusts.

"Babies?"

And then it burst on his brain. Oh, God, with all this talk of a takeover, he'd completely forgotten. Evan groaned.

He groaned even louder when he saw her. Claire was standing in the doorway, her eyes narrow, the look on her face far from tolerant. She was holding Rachel.

"Did you forget something?"

Chapter Four

The very next moment, Libby came bounding into the room like the first volley of fireworks at a Fourth of July celebration. She immediately attached herself to Evan and began talking as if she were trying to outrace a hurricane, her speed accelerating with each word.

"Did you forget about Rachel? Mama said you did. I thought maybe you wanted us to have her. I'd like a little sister, but Mama says she has to be married first this time. And she says we're fine, just us, but we can be finer if we have Rachel. So, do you wanna give us Rachel?"

"Libby, hush." Claire placed her hand on the little girl's shoulder to draw her back. She noted that Evan looked dazed, as if he'd fallen headfirst into a whirlpool.

Shaking off the effects of the blitzkrieg attack, Evan crossed to Claire. His legs felt wooden, as did his brain. How could he have forgotten to go home to pick up Rachel?

Easy, because it wasn't something he was accustomed to doing or even thinking about. He thought of very little else whenever he was immersed in work, certainly not a child he'd just acquired in the past twenty-four hours.

"I am really very sorry." The feeble words of apology crashed and broke up like pitifully small waves upon the shore of her annoyance. He tried again because, although he hated the fact, he did owe her an explanation. "I did forget," he admitted, glancing at Libby, "but I'm in the middle of a hostile takeover here."

"Damn straight you are," Claire retorted, "as of right now."

If he thought he could turn those gorgeous eyes on her and melt her resolve just because there was a hint of contrition within their green lights, he was in for a surprise. She was long past being taken in by good-looking men with faces like moody poets' and bodies like determined athletes'. He wasn't going to get away with this trick.

"We had a temporary arrangement, mister, not a permanent one." She held Rachel out to him. "Your daughter, Mr. Quartermain."

Every time he heard that description, it was like a knife twisting in his gut. "She's not—"

Oh, no, he wasn't going to get out of it by playing with words. Rachel was his, all right. "She's your responsibility," Claire emphasized.

It was Devin who had always been the ladies' man when they were growing up, but Evan had picked up a few things along the way just by listening. He gave it a shot. After all, he had nothing to lose and peace and quiet to gain.

"Oh, but you were doing so well." Uttered with forced feeling, the words fell flat.

She'd had her inoculations against flattery, as well, and far better flattery than what he seemed to be capable of. "If that's your idea of charm, you have a lot of work ahead of you."

Giving up the charade, Evan played it straight and was

himself again. And a desperate self it was, too. "Look, what do you want me to do? I'm at work."

Claire shifted Rachel to her other hip and took the stapler out of Libby's hands before her daughter could staple herself to Evan's chair.

"Well, for starters, you can stop being at work all the time." She punctuated her statement by depositing the stapler on top of his desk. Hard.

He stared at her. Was she crazy? "You're suggesting I quit?"

Why did he have to think in such exaggerated terms? Claire blew out a breath. "I'm suggesting you take some time off."

He thought of the extended meeting, and Donovan's long list of things he wanted him to look into before the next one. "Now?"

He sounded as if she were asking him to abdicate the throne of England instead of taking a few days off. Claire went toe-to-toe with him, refusing to be intimidated by his high-and-mighty tone.

"Right now. You do have time coming to you, don't you?"

"Mr. Quartermain has a great deal of time accrued," Alma volunteered, hoping to be helpful.

Evan glared at his secretary. Why was the woman still here, listening to all this? Didn't she have anything better to do?

Claire nodded, satisfied. Just as she thought. "And he's going to begin unaccruing it."

Her declaration sent Evan over the top. He wasn't about to do anything of the kind. "Just who do you think you are, coming in here, ordering me around—?"

Claire had a feeling that, given the chance, he could be every bit as verbose as Libby, and a hell of a lot more pompous. She wasn't about to give him that chance. "I'm the woman you left your baby with."

He clenched his hands at his sides to keep from throttling her in front of witnesses. "I already told you, she is not my baby."

And that was another thing; she was sick of his denials. Hearing them brought back the sound of Jack's voice when he had questioned Libby's paternity. As if she'd even look at another man when she thought herself in love with him. Scratch the surface and men were all the same, scrambling away to save their worthless, scrawny necks. When she thought of the fact that she, abandoned and alone, would have killed to have a family, and Evan was trying to throw his away, she could have strangled him.

She fixed him with a look that made him want to squirm even though he wasn't guilty of anything.

"Can you honestly look at Rachel and say she's not yours?" She looked from the baby to Evan. Like two drawings from the same brush. How could he find it in his heart to deny her her birthright? "Honestly?"

He heard the little sigh coming from the doorway. Evan raised his eyes to Alma, his meaning clear.

The woman instantly began backing out. "I'll just go see about making arrangements for some vacation time," she murmured, disappearing.

Oh, no, this was going to get back to Donovan. He could feel a noose tightening around his neck.

"I can't take any time off," Evan called after the woman.

Claire blocked him with her body, managing to slip in between him and the doorjamb. "Oh, yes, you can and you should and you will."

Libby tugged on his jacket before he could tell Claire exactly what he thought of her instructions. And before he could bank down the very powerful pull he'd just felt as his body had brushed against Claire's in the struggle to gain the doorway.

Having to answer the child took his mind off the woman. "What?"

Libby looked up at him with a solemnity reserved for those far older than she. "You better listen to her when she talks like that," Libby advised. "That's Mama's mad voice."

Evan's eyebrows narrowed as he glared at Claire. Things were bad enough right now without having to deal with an overbearing woman. "Maybe she'd like to hear *my* mad voice."

"I have," Libby confided to her mother, "but it's really not so bad."

Claire didn't know if Libby was actually trying to be a peacemaker or just talking, but she did know that the effort would be wasted on Evan.

"Libby, please be quiet. This is between Mr. Quartermain and me."

Libby frowned. It seemed very obvious to her that they had forgotten someone.

"And Rachel. Don't forget Rachel," she urged, looking from her mother to Mr. Q., which was as much of the man's name as she could manage easily.

Libby succeeded where her mother failed. She made him feel ashamed of himself. He was completely forgetting Rachel, and that hadn't been his intent. He wanted her taken care of, even if she wasn't his; he just didn't want his entire world to be put through the wringer in order to do it.

Claire could see the difference in him instantly. There were signs of remorse, however faint. She lightened her intense assault. Maybe she was coming on too strong, not so much for Rachel's sake, which would have been excusable, but because Evan Quartermain made her think of Jack. She hated being unfair.

"She's right, you know," Claire agreed quietly. "You did forget. We both did."

That she should include herself surprised Evan. "Yes, I know," he snapped, then flushed. It wasn't her he was really angry with; it was circumstances. And perhaps himself. "Sorry, it's just that this isn't really a good time for me to be taking any days off."

The man seemed to be completely married to his career. When had he had the time to create this delightful, wet little bundle?

"It's the age of the computer," Claire reminded him needlessly. "It can seem as if you're right here, except that you'll really be there. At home. With Rachel," she emphasized in case he missed that.

She couldn't begin to understand, he thought. Telecommuting just wasn't the same thing. "But I can't just—"

He blew out a breath. If he tried, he supposed he could make it work, at least part of the time. He had enough access codes and enough information to do the work on any desktop. Maybe he could take a few days off to get this all straightened out.

Besides, what choice did he have? It was either let Rachel remain with him or have family services take her. Even if the latter was easier, he had this nagging feeling that he shouldn't give her up so quickly.

Claire knew that she should have her head examined, but she felt sorry for him. He looked like a man who was hopelessly trapped. Maybe he couldn't exude charm very well, but he did lost-and-trapped to a T.

Knowing she was really going to regret this, she tendered an offer. "Look, I'll make a deal with you. You make an effort here, take some time off, at least learn which end is supposed to be diapered and which is supposed to be fed, and I'll see what I can do about taking up the slack."

He hadn't expected her to volunteer, not after he'd left

her high and dry last night. And not after she'd made it perfectly clear that he couldn't buy his way into her services any longer.

Evan stared at her, wishing he could figure her out. But even if he couldn't understand her, he could understand that she was coming to his rescue.

"You will?"

Uh-oh, she knew that look. Claire was quick to head him off at the pass before he went galloping off in the wrong direction.

"Slack," she repeated. "As in loose hours, not as in twenty-four. Got it, Mr. Quartermain?"

"Got it. Completely," he swore, in case she thought he was going to renege again. He was grateful for the help. It meant that, at least for a while, he wasn't going to have to go poring over the telephone directory, trying to locate a nanny on short notice.

He looked at Claire hopefully as Libby wiggled farther into his chair, whizzing around. "So, you'll take her back home now?" Very gingerly, he lifted Libby out of his swivel chair. She'd spent the past few minutes spinning around in it, pushing herself along against his desk with her feet to gain momentum. To his surprise, Libby didn't protest.

"And you'll arrive shortly in my wake?" Claire asked. She caught Libby's hand as she took an uncertain step. The little girl grinned up at her foolishly. Libby was dizzy, Claire thought.

The terms were not negotiable, and he knew it. Not with that look in her eyes. He was sure it was the same one Churchill had had in his eyes when he'd delivered his speech on the floor of parliament about fighting the enemy on the beaches.

"I'll be in your wake," he promised. Libby had shifted back to his side, curling her fingers around his hand again and smiling up at him as if he was her new best friend. Just what he needed. He extracted his hand.

"Shortly?" Claire emphasized, her eyes on his.

He had the uncomfortable feeling that she would know if he tried to lie or put her off. So he didn't. "I've got to talk to my boss."

"You have a boss?" Libby asked incredulously, emphasizing each word. "Mama is her own boss."

He didn't wonder. "That's because no one can tell your mama what to do."

Claire knew Evan didn't mean it as a compliment, but she wasn't after compliments from this man. She just wanted him to do what was right.

She smiled at him serenely. "I'm glad we understand each other." She caught Libby by the shoulder before she could get into exploring anything else, specifically the floor-to-ceiling shelves she seemed to have her eye on. "Now, we'll get out of your way. We'll be at my house, waiting for you." Just in case he had any ideas about a repeat performance of yesterday, she added, "But don't think that I'd hesitate in coming back here again if you don't show up."

He was beginning to fully appreciate exactly what he was up against. "Not for a minute." Evan paused, studying her. He had to know. "Are you an army brat?"

She had no idea where the question came from. "No, why?"

To him, it was obvious. "You give orders like a drill sergeant."

Yeah, well, there was a reason for that, she thought. "Comes from having to take care of myself at an early age." Her father, a widowed, sought-after neurosurgeon, had hardly ever seemed to be home. The housekeeper he'd employed did little to fill the void in her life. Claire had been left on her own a great deal.

Turning, Claire let him get the door. With Libby's hand firmly in hers, she ushered her daughter out before her. Rachel began fussing. It was time for another bottle, Claire thought.

"We'll be waiting for you," she said pointedly as she passed Alma's desk.

"I've got Mr. Donovan on the telephone," Alma informed Evan, watching the entourage file by to the elevator. She shook her head in disbelief.

"What would I do without you, Alma?" Evan muttered, turning on his heel.

"I was just about to get into the car again," Claire told Evan.

She shut the door behind him as he walked into her living room. It had been over three hours since she'd left him in the office, and the whole scenario was beginning to play like déjà vu.

Well, at least he'd managed to avert that disaster, he thought. He watched as another female came hurrying toward him. Libby wrapped herself around his leg, greeting him as if they were old friends.

Old was the word for it, he thought. Suddenly, he felt ancient, with the weight of the world on his shoulders, not to mention around his leg.

"I had a couple of emergencies to handle before I could get away," he told Claire.

"You can sit down here, by me," Libby told him, giving him no choice as she yanked on his arm. Evan found himself sitting on the sofa, in front of a tape of six-foot dancing squirrels who were also singing. Badly.

"You have an emergency here," Claire told him evenly. "Remember?"

The squirrels were extolling the virtues of always being kind, even to people who were mean to you. Maybe the woman responded to kindness, Evan thought. He did his best to smile. "Yes, but I left that one in capable hands."

Suppressing a grin, she turned down the sound on the television. "Your charming is getting better, but it still isn't good enough to make me take Rachel for the night."

"The night?" Evan repeated dumbly. He hadn't even thought about that possibility.

Claire nodded. "The night. Bedtime." Her mouth curved in response to the look on his face. "You know, the time that separates the parents from those who haven't been so blessed."

Blessed wasn't exactly the word he would have used. "Bedtime." His mouth was suddenly dry. Evan's eyes shifted to the baby, and then back to Claire. "Any chance?"

There was a hint of panic in his eyes, and she tried not to laugh. Above all, she remained firm. "Not even in hell."

She couldn't just leave him alone with the baby. He had no idea what to do. "Claire, you're so much better than I am at this."

There was no way he was going to talk her into it, or his way out of it.

"Ever hear of 'practice makes perfect'?" And then, because he truly did look lost, she relented. A little. "I tell you what, I'll spend the day with you in your house, coaching you through everything. By nightfall, you'll be an expert." She knew that was really stretching it. "Or at least you won't break her."

Well, it was something. He nodded, taking out his checkbook. "All right, just let me make out a check for you."

Was there a price on everything for this man? Hadn't he learned yet? She struggled not to let her temper get the better of her. "Did I say I was charging you for this?"

Why was she getting so steamed? "No, but I just assumed—"

That was his first mistake. "Never, ever assume anything with me, Mr. Quartermain," Claire warned. "You'll find that you're usually wrong." She set him straight. "I'm doing this because Rachel needs someone in her corner. And because you are the most pathetic-looking would-be father I've ever seen." He bristled slightly, and she bit her tongue to keep from laughing. "But at least you are a would-be father and you get points for that."

He didn't understand. Right now, he felt as if there was very little he *could* understand. "Points?"

She waved the word away. She hadn't meant to let him so far into her private life. "Just an expression." Making a mental inventory of the things he was going to need, she picked Rachel up. "Okay, let's go get your feet wet."

Libby's eyes danced with excitement as she hopped to her feet. "Are we going swimming, Mama?"

Claire laughed, and the soft sound seemed to waft under his skin. "Only if we forget to change Rachel's diapers for too long."

Evan groaned.

"Here, I thought you might need this."

Evan opened his eyes. It took him a moment to focus on what Claire was holding. Completely exhausted after being mercilessly drilled for what seemed like an eternity, he'd sought a moment's respite on the sofa while Claire had gone to warm yet another bottle for the bottomless pit who was masquerading as a baby.

"It's coffee." She pressed the mug into his hand. She'd found the brew in his kitchen and decided that he might need it to fortify him for the night ahead.

Evan took the mug in both hands, afraid he might drop it otherwise. He felt more tired now than he'd been after the marathon meeting last night. "Oh, I was sort of hoping it was hemlock."

With Rachel temporarily occupied, Claire sat down next to Evan on the sofa, sidling into the small space beside him. "You're not doing that bad."

He felt a little jolt and wondered if it was the caffeine sinking in or the effects of the thigh brushing against his arm as Claire took her place.

"Matter of opinion," he muttered. He took a long sip, then studied her over the rim of the mug. Why was she here? Why was she helping him? He was nothing to her. Evan decided that it was because she liked ordering people around. She'd done her fair share with him this afternoon. "Something you seem to have a lot of."

She took it in stride. "I'm not a shy wallflower, if that's what you mean. Wallflowers have a habit of being flattened and covered with wallpaper or paint if they're not careful."

In an odd sort of way, he actually followed that. Evan decided he was getting really punchy. They had been at this most of the afternoon. It was an endless circle of feeding, burping, changing, rocking and feeding again. Very little sleep seemed to be working its way into the pattern. He fervently hoped it meant that Rachel was going to sleep through the night.

For a drill sergeant, she made a good cup of coffee, he thought, draining his mug before setting it down. "I pity the person who tried to flatten you."

Sometimes, she talked too much. "I wasn't speaking from experience," she said stiffly.

He shrugged. Maybe he'd misunderstood. "Sorry, I just assumed—"

Claire shook her head, but there was a smile on her lips. "There you go again. I told you not to assume anything about me."

Maybe it was because he was tired, but she piqued his curiosity. "All right, then I'll ask."

She regarded him cautiously. "Go ahead, maybe I'll even answer."

She had skeletons in her closet, he guessed. He glanced at Libby, who was sitting down for a change. He'd never seen so much energy in one small body before. But for the moment, she seemed content in rocking Rachel's swing, and Rachel, mercifully, was actually dozing. It looked promising for tonight.

"Libby mentioned something about you saying that this time you'd be married before you had a daughter. What did she mean?"

Claire had hoped that he hadn't picked up on that. Enough time had elapsed since Libby's unfortunate comment for Claire to think he hadn't heard.

She squared her shoulders unconsciously. It reminded Evan of someone preparing for battle.

"If you're asking me if I'm married, I think the answer is obvious. No. If you're asking me if I was married when Libby was born, the answer is the same. No." She dared him to make something of it or, worse, offer inane words of pity.

He did neither, but he did make an educated guess. "He ran out on you."

Her expression hardened. "I don't see that as any of your business." Claire paused. Now she was sounding just like him. Besides, she had nothing to be ashamed of. If there was shame, it belonged to Jack. "So fast you could see smoke coming from his shoes." She smiled without humor. "Seems his 'undying love' had a very short life expectancy."

Claire seemed to shrug the matter off as inconsequential. But if it was, he thought, it wouldn't have bothered her that he'd asked.

"We're better off without him," she finished.

It was hard not to miss the bitterness. "Do you tell Libby that?"

Was he actually trying to preach to her? "No, I tell her we're managing just fine." She was very careful not to taint Libby's views, even at this age. "There's a difference."

Not that he could see. "Semantics."

"Semantics makes a difference," she insisted patiently, because he was obviously too dumb to see it on his own. "This way, she doesn't get the impression I hate her father."

He tried to envision her hating someone and wondered why he should care one way or another. Just idle curiosity, nothing more. "Do you?"

"No." It was an honest answer. "I pity him. He missed an awful lot by being selfish." Claire grinned as she looked toward her daughter. "More for me."

He would have said it was a case of sour grapes if he hadn't seen her expression. She was serious. But how could she be? She was a single parent, and it was clear what a nightmare that could be. "Like worries about bills and sleepless nights?"

"That's part of it," she agreed, "but not all of it. Not by a long shot. He missed the thrill of seeing something of his—that was meaningful," she added, "growing. He missed first words, missed the hugs, missed sloppy kisses with so much heart behind them, they burst your own." Her eyes were shining as she enumerated. "That far outweighs anything else, believe me."

"I almost can," he marveled. He wasn't tired anymore. Evan sat up, looking at her. "You sound like you actually love being a mother."

She did. "Can't think of anything I love better."

He had one for her. "How about being successful?"

Claire grinned. She doubted that he could understand, but maybe he could. Someday. "Haven't you heard? I am.

I've raised a great kid, and the process is still in progress. This is success, Mr. Quartermain—'' she gestured toward Libby ''—not stemming the tide of hostile takeovers.''

That was a direct criticism. The gap that had momentarily narrowed between them widened again. "Your opinion.''

''Yes, it is, and it should be yours.'' It was his loss if it wasn't. ''But to each his own.''

She uncurled her legs, which seemed remarkably long, given the fact that she only came up to his shoulder.

''Well, Libby and I have to be getting back,'' she said.

Panic returned in spades. He was on his feet in an instant. ''You're leaving?''

She laughed. ''Just the house, not town,'' she assured him. ''We'll be just next door.'' Picking up a pencil from the coffee table, she wrote down her telephone number on the side of his television guide. ''Here's my number. Call if you need me.''

He barely looked at it. He was looking at her instead. ''I don't have to.''

This was a surprise. ''That confident?''

He shook his head, fighting the impulse to grab her arm and plead with her to stay. ''No, I need you now. Here.''

Claire ignored the way the words he used made a small knot form in her stomach. Instead, she made light of it and fluttered her lashes. ''Why, Mr. Quartermain, we scarcely know one another.''

Chapter Five

It took Evan a moment to gather his thoughts together. When she fluttered her lashes like that at him, it made him forget what he was going to say. Not that he fell for the mock flirtation—it was just that the fluttering drew his attention to her eyes, and she did have beautiful eyes. Big, lustrous blue eyes that made a man's mind wander.

The tiny salvo of panic fired the next minute had his mind returning quickly enough. He glanced at Rachel. She was dozing now, but for how long?

"No, really." Forgetting himself, he caught hold of Claire's wrist. "I don't feel qualified enough to stay alone with her."

Then, realizing what he was doing, he released her as if her wrist had suddenly turned red-hot.

She remembered how lost she'd felt coming home from the hospital with Libby. So lost that no map in the world could have found her. But it passed, and what made it pass was getting comfortable in her role.

There was encouragement in her eyes as she smiled at

him. ''No one feels qualified the first time around.'' Maybe she should have thought that it served him right. You play, you pay. But somehow, she really didn't feel as if he deserved the sentiment. At least he was trying, which was more than Jack had ever done when he found himself faced with fatherhood. ''Think of this as a trial by fire.''

Yeah, and he was the one going down in flames. Evan could see it in her expression. She wasn't going to budge. Well, he wasn't going to beg. If Claire wasn't going to remain here of her own free will or because her conscience was making her, he refused to humble himself by begging.

Even though he wanted to.

Damn it, she was a woman—she was supposed to feel guilty about leaving an inexperienced, hapless man alone with a small baby. Hadn't she read her basic instruction manual?

Okay, if this was the way she wanted to play it, so be it. Evan squared his shoulders, an about-to-be-executed man laughing at the gallows.

''Sure, how hard can it be?'' he asked rhetorically, stealing another glance at Rachel.

The baby looked to be still dozing. Maybe she'd sleep right through to morning. A bud of hope began to bloom. He knew the right thing would be to place her in her crib, but he wasn't, for all the money in the world, about to take her out of that swing while her eyes were closed. The saying ''Let sleeping dogs lie'' applied twice over to babies.

''That's the spirit,'' Claire said, cheering him on.

It was a crock and they both knew it, but she was afraid that if Evan asked her to remain again, if he looked at her with those sad, liquid green eyes, she would cave in. And she couldn't. She had Libby to think of and way too much to do. As it was, she'd let almost two days slide because of this man and his baby. She had a life, too, and it was time she got back to it.

Crossing to her daughter, she extended her hand. "C'mon, Libby," Claire whispered so as not to wake the baby, "we've got to get going now."

Libby stood up. As she was led away, she looked uncertainly over her shoulder at the sleeping Rachel. "Can we take her?"

Claire had expected this. It amazed her how attached Libby could get in such a short time. Like her mother, she thought ruefully. Not the best trait to pass on to a daughter in this day and age.

"No, we can't take her," Claire told her patiently. "Mr. Quartermain's going to be taking care of her now."

"Him?" There was no mistaking the surprise and doubt in Libby's voice.

That was exactly how he felt, Evan thought. Even a four-year-old could see he wasn't qualified. So why couldn't the four-year-old's mother see that?

He looked at Claire, hoping she'd have a change of heart.

"He'll be fine." Claire scooted Libby to the door, but she was looking at Evan when she said it. Doubt nagged at her.

Libby was no help. "I'm not tired, Mama," she announced, digging in her heels at the front door. "Can't we stay and help some more?"

Yes, can't you? Evan begged silently, looking at Claire. He knew he'd promised himself not to beg, but he figured doing it silently didn't really count.

"No, we can't." Claire was firm.

Evan was never going to learn if she took over, and she couldn't always be here. He didn't even *like* her, for pity's sake. Still, Claire found she had to battle herself, as well as Libby, just to get out the door.

Turning in the doorway, she struggled not to give in. "Okay, don't lose the number." She pointed to it on the table.

A hell of a lot of good the number would do him. She probably wouldn't even answer when he called. "I won't," he muttered.

He made her smile and reminded her of a child trying hard to pretend he wasn't afraid of the dark, fearfully eyeing the light switch as his parent's hand hovered over it. Impulsively, wanting to offer him a bit of comfort, Claire brushed a kiss to his cheek.

Evan jerked his head in surprise, and the kiss ended with a brief, unexpected and jolting touch of lips. Hers to his.

Claire stepped back, flustered and...unsettled, she supposed. She certainly hadn't meant for that to happen. But now that it had...

Without thinking, she ran the tip of her tongue along the outline of her lips, tasting him. Drawing in the flavor.

There were a thousand tiny angels in toe shoes whirling up and down her arms. She took a deep breath before saying anything.

"You'll do fine," she repeated in a whisper.

"Yeah, right," he muttered.

Or thought he did. Maybe he'd just formed the words in his mind. Evan blinked, trying to clear his head. She was standing two feet away from him, as if that minimal contact had propelled them apart with the same intensity that incurring thirty thousand volts of electricity would have done. His brain certainly felt as if it had just been zapped.

His eyes narrowed as Evan tried to comprehend what had just happened. "Did you just kiss me?" he asked. Or had he just experienced a temporary lapse of consciousness?

"On the cheek, for luck," Claire said a bit too quickly. "You jumped," she explained, wanting it to be very clear just how these circumstances had come about.

A mistake, that's all it was. A mistake, nothing more. He was relieved. And somehow disappointed.

He was tired—that's what he was, he told himself.

"It's been a hard day," he mumbled. Hell of a pitiful excuse for acting like a skittish virginal maiden in a morality play. Claire probably thought he was some kind of an inexperienced dolt who'd created a baby his first time at bat because he didn't know what he was doing.

For two cents, he'd show her he knew what he was doing. Right here, right now, acting under the least bit of provocation, he'd take her into his arms and show her that he could kiss a woman senseless if he chose. Well, maybe not right now—there were kids to put to bed first....

Evan dragged his hand through his hair. What a mess, he thought, exasperated.

A smile began to curl from the tips of her toes, winding its way through her body like a fresh, fragrant summer breeze, conquering the terrain it passed through.

She wasn't altogether sure just what had happened here, but she knew she liked it. And she definitely liked his flavor. Dark, manly. She pressed her lips together to savor it again before nodding. "All right, then, we're off."

Libby's hand in hers, she half led, half dragged the girl out the door.

Evan remained rooted to the spot, wondering if he was losing his mind. Wondering if wondering about it meant that he had already lost it.

And wondering what it would be like to kiss her in earnest instead of by mistake.

He didn't stand there wondering for long. As soon as the door closed, Rachel's mouth opened. A lusty cry emerged, made that much more powerful because she'd rested up for it.

It snared Evan's attention immediately, banishing everything else to the background.

"Oh, God."

* * *

Claire heard the cries through the door. She heard Evan's response, as well. For a long moment, she wavered, torn between coming to his rescue and sticking to her guns.

She did have things to do, she reasoned sternly, and she couldn't spend all her waking hours holding Evan's hand.

Not that holding his hand would exactly come under the heading of unpleasant hardships.

Upbraiding herself, Claire kept walking. She'd put in a long day on the heels of an endless night. She needed her rest, too. Besides, she couldn't get involved with a man who might or might not be involved with another woman who in turn was the mother of a child who might or might not be his.

It was too complicated to sort out tonight.

Libby looked over her shoulder at Evan's house the entire way. "Aren't we going to help him?" she asked mournfully.

Almost as mournful, Claire thought, as Evan probably was right now.

"We are," she said firmly, unlocking her door. "By letting him help himself." She ushered Libby in and closed the door. Claire tossed her purse on the side table. "He's not going to learn how to take care of Rachel unless he does it by himself."

Libby wasn't convinced. Mr. Q. had looked funny when they left. Like his tummy hurt or something. "What if he breaks her?"

"Then he'll call."

That made sense to Libby.

Evan wanted to call. A dozen times or so, he had wanted to call. He had even gone so far as to punch in six of the seven digits of Claire's telephone number on two different occasions before he let the receiver drop back into the cradle.

No, damn it, he wasn't going to break down. He wasn't going to give that woman the satisfaction of calling her and asking for help. He had two master's degrees, for heaven's sakes, gotten simultaneously—while working. Better than anyone else, he knew what it meant to be under pressure. Hell, he thrived on pressure.

He could do this.

He couldn't do this, he thought miserably several hours later.

Pressure was one thing, but none of the pressure he'd ever been under had meant being knee-deep in diapers. Evan felt like a man sleepwalking through a nightmare.

For lack of a changing table, and with a sense of horror as to what any leaks might do to the polished finish on his antique desk or his coffee table, Evan had Rachel lying on a blanket on his bed when he changed her diaper.

"Doesn't any of this stuff stay inside of you?" he asked as he took off yet another soggy, misshapen wrapper. He'd lost count as to how many.

There was no pattern to it, either. Rachel needed to be changed before she ate, after she ate and when she didn't eat at all.

He set the bottle of talcum powder aside and looked at her accusingly. "You spit up, you discharge—are you sure you're not hollow?"

Rachel responded by kicking her chubby little legs so hard, the tab on the diaper ripped off just as he was trying to close its mate. It hung there at her hip, useless.

"Great."

Force of habit had him looking at the clock on his nightstand. It was a little past four in the morning. By his reckoning, he'd gotten in about five and a half minutes of sleep since Claire had, with malice aforethought, cruelly abandoned him.

"We're down to our last four diapers. You'd better learn some bladder control, young lady—or I'd better get smart and start investing in the company that makes these things."

As he spoke, Rachel stared at him with mesmerized eyes. If he didn't know any better, Evan would have said that she understood every word.

Which was absurd.

Absurd, huh? So what did that make him? He was the one talking to her as if she understood.

With a frustrated sigh, he slipped one of the last remaining diapers under her bottom. He tossed the useless diaper into the corner, on top of the others. Hidden beneath was a wastepaper basket long since full. He meant to throw it out when he got the chance. Probably sometime in the next month.

This was becoming old hat to him, he realized dully as he fastened the tabs in place again. At least he was getting faster at it.

Mercifully, Rachel refrained from executing any high kicks, and the diaper held.

"There, try to keep it dry for more than five minutes, okay?"

Picking her up again, he made his way back into the spare bedroom. The one that had been turned into a makeshift nursery. As gently as possible, Evan laid Rachel down in the crib, then backed away.

He made it all the way to the threshold before Rachel began to cry.

Evan cringed, but remained where he was. "I don't care," he told her. "Hear me? Cry all you want, I'm leaving."

To demonstrate, he shut off the light and closed the door firmly behind him.

Rachel continued crying.

With the determination of a man who knew in his heart that he was right, Evan went to his room, shut the door and crawled into bed.

The sound of her cries followed him, seeping through the crack under the door.

Desperate for some sleep, Evan pulled his pillow over his head and tried to think of something, anything, that would help him block out the noise.

His mind was a blank.

And then he thought of Claire. Of the sweet sting of her lips as they'd suddenly touched his. He could almost feel them now as he lay there in the dark. They were soft, silky, as light as a butterfly as they passed over his mouth.

This wasn't any good.

He tried to think of something else.

And couldn't.

One way or another, that Walker woman was going to kill him, he thought grudgingly. Muttering a barrage of choice words, Evan threw off the blanket and stormed back into the hallway.

Was it his imagination, or had Rachel's cries increased in volume? They seemed to be rattling the very fillings in his teeth. He could certainly feel them vibrating in his chest.

What had he ever done to deserve this?

If he had any brains in his head, he would just turn around and walk away again. Or better yet, get in his car and—

What was he thinking? That would be abandonment. And Rachel had already been abandoned once in her young life. Nobody deserved that.

Feeling like a condemned man who was damned no matter what he did, Evan swung open the door to her room and stumbled over to Rachel's Portacrib in the dark.

The thought that she needed a better place to sleep

slipped in and out of his head in less time than it took to form the words. Maybe he should look into getting a real crib. Temporarily.

"Okay, okay, you win. I'm here," he told her, grinding out the words. She howled louder. Chagrined, he lowered his voice. "Shh—shh—shh," he soothed, "it's okay."

Bending over, he scooped her up, careful to keep one hand beneath her neck, cradling Rachel's head the way Claire had showed him.

"Hell of a way for the fastest-rising executive at Donovan Digital Incorporated to wind up," he told her, but his voice was soft and there was no animosity. Just stupefied wonder.

Rachel snuffled, hiccuping before she finally stopped crying. Evan saw the tracks of her tears shining along her cheeks as he brought her into the hallway. Guilt pierced him as cleanly as if it had been wielding a knife.

She couldn't help crying, he thought. She didn't know any better. At six months or so, Rachel was too young to know how to manipulate a man. Unlike some women.

He looked down into her face and felt himself smiling. "It's been more than a year since I spent all night in the company of a female. Wouldn't you know, it has to be someone who's small enough to fit into my sink."

Evan could have sworn Rachel smiled at him. Maybe it was just gas. He tucked her against his shoulder. And then he felt something, something that wasn't damp for a change, spreading out along his chest, laying claim to his heart.

Shrugging, he tried to ignore it as he walked downstairs and into the living room. Resigning himself to his ordeal, Evan turned on the stereo. He might as well listen to music as he paced.

Claire woke with a start.
Pulling her clock over, she held it as she waited for her

eyes to focus. It was nearly six. She'd overslept, she thought, putting the clock down again. Since she was accustomed to rising at five, anything beyond that felt like sleeping in. And felt sinfully indulgent.

Claire stretched, and then it dawned on her. Evan hadn't called. She had expected the telephone to be ringing off the hook all night, and he hadn't called. Not once.

Swinging her legs off the bed, she picked up the telephone. There was a dial tone. Concerned, she checked the button on the side, but the ringer was on. If anyone had called, she would have heard it.

Which meant that Evan hadn't called.

Now she was really worried. She should have never left him alone with Rachel. God only knew what had happened there last night. Any scenarios she called up, Claire abandoned half-formed. It was a lot better not to second-guess in this case.

Claire got dressed as quickly as possible. It took a little longer to do the same for Libby. The little girl, who was always fully awake the instant her eyes opened, wiggled with excitement as she anticipated seeing Rachel again. Claire chatted nonsense with her, not wanting to alarm Libby needlessly. It was bad enough that she was worried.

"Will it be our turn to have Rachel tonight?" Libby pressed eagerly as Claire tied her sneakers. "He got to play with her last night."

Claire could just hear Evan's reaction to Libby's assessment of what he had gone through. "I don't think he'd call it playing, Lib."

Throwing a jacket around Libby's shoulders to ward off the November cold, Claire didn't bother grabbing anything for herself. Her agitation was keeping her warm enough. With Libby leading the way, she hurried out of the house and cut across the driveways.

If anything had happened to Rachel, it would be all her fault, she thought, ringing the bell.

There was no answer.

She tried again, leaning on the bell. Nothing.

Claire felt a tightness in her throat as she urgently pressed her thumb against the tiny white button a third time.

The door finally opened just as Claire was debating forcing open a window.

She caught herself staring. Evan Quartermain looked like hell. His hair, which had always been so perfectly combed, with each hair in place, was mussed as if he'd been wrestling—and lost. It hung in his eyes, giving him a little-boy look. A very lost, disheveled little boy.

There were stains on both shoulders of his expensive salmon-colored shirt, as well as stains trailing down one sleeve and across the front. The shirt was pulled out of his gray trousers, which, after putting up a good fight, had surrendered their razor-sharp creases. They were as rumpled as anything that might have been pulled off a clearance rack at a discount store.

It looked as if he had been in a fight, and she knew who the victor had been. It was difficult keeping the grin off her face, but she managed. Mostly. "You slept in your clothes?"

"Who slept? She's worse than that mechanical bunny." Stepping back, Evan continued rocking Rachel against him. By now, it was an ingrained, automatic motion. He sighed. "She's even got more energy than your kid."

Libby, whom Claire had barely managed to restrain from bouncing into his house, now stood in awe of the disheveled man in the doorway. She hung on to Claire's jeans as she looked up at him.

He was a pretty frightening sight, Claire thought. And rather endearing for all that. He seemed...more real now.

Claire closed the door he had left standing open. "You look like you had a hell of a night."

He blinked. The sunlight in the room registered for the first time. He'd been in a dense fog for the past couple of hours. Maybe more.

"You mean it's morning?"

This time, she did laugh. "Yes, you made it. You spent the night in the haunted castle and you survived." He looked as if he was going to drop at any minute. She had visions of him flattening Rachel. "Here," she said, holding out her hands, "let me take her."

It felt as if half his brain had shut down. Evan stared first at Claire, then down at himself and the baby he held against him. "I'm not sure my arms can open anymore."

And here she thought he couldn't exaggerate. Shaking her head, Claire slowly made the transfer, taking Rachel from him. She automatically cupped her hand around the baby's bottom.

"Hey, dry." She looked at Evan. "I'm impressed."

His eyes kept insisting on closing. He had to struggle to keep them open. "And I'm running on empty." He had something to tell her. What was it? That thoughts of her mouth had haunted him all night? No, that wasn't it. Although they had. Dry, she'd said something about dry. Diapers, that was it. Diapers. "There aren't any diapers left. She used them all."

It was to be expected. "I've got one more box in my car."

He grinned as if she'd just said his stock had split. "You're a saint."

"Wow, you are punchy." Claire hooked one arm through his, still holding Rachel. "C'mon, let's put you to bed."

Evan took a deep, fortifying breath before trying to make his feet work. He stumbled after her. "Is that an offer?"

When he heard them, he had no idea where the words had come from. Maybe he was even hallucinating them.

He'd thought about it enough during the night. Finding out what it would be like having her in bed with him, yielding to him instead of sparring with him.

Claire faltered, recovering almost instantly. My, my, but still waters did run deep.

"No, that's an order," she replied calmly. One step at a time, she pulled him up the stairs. "You know, the things I'm good at giving." Finally on the landing, she looked around. "This way?" she guessed, nodding toward the right.

His legs were no longer functioning. He wasn't even sure if he felt them. "Just leave me here—I can stretch out on the floor."

She laughed, tugging on his arm. The door to the room she'd indicated was standing open. She was right; it was his. And it was in a state of complete chaos, which meant it matched the rest of the house.

"It's not that bad," she told him.

Her denial was like a final rallying cry. Evan drew himself up. "Want to bet? I didn't have any sleep last night. Or the night before, either. At least, not much."

It felt as if he'd always been awake. Always stumbling through life.

Very gently, she led him to his bed. The blanket was a mess. For the time being, she pushed it to one side. "Welcome to parenthood."

"But she's not—" It was a feeble protest that died before it was completed.

"I know, I know." Exerting very little force, she pushed him onto the bed. He collapsed like a tower of limp laundry. "Shut up and get some sleep."

His eyes were already shutting again. "You'll be here when I wake up?" he mumbled.

From somewhere in the distance, her voice floated back to him. "I'll be here when you wake up. This was the slack I was talking about."

He didn't have any strength to say another word, or even to rue the fact that he'd been laid low by someone who weighed less than his television set. He hardly ever talked in his sleep.

Chapter Six

It curled around him slowly, nudging him to consciousness bit by bit. The scent of coffee mixed with the fragrance of spring.

Vaguely, Evan remembered that it wasn't spring. Halloween and strangely dressed children with pumpkins and pillowcases, begging for candy, had gone by. It was fall, almost winter.

Increments of facts sprinkled through his brain like light morning drizzle, melding with the scent. But it was the sound that woke him.

Or rather, the lack of it.

There was no buzzing in his ears, no persistent wailing.

Evan opened his eyes, listening, wondering if it had all been just a bad dream. The baby, the mess, the sleepless night. Just a bad dream.

And then he looked down at his rumpled clothes and knew that it wasn't. It was all too real. Someone had left him a baby and called him a father. And the blonde next door had abandoned him.

With a sigh that was one part weariness and two parts resignation, Evan sat up and dragged both hands through his hair, trying to come to. There was no doubt in his mind that this was what it felt like to be run over by an eighteen-wheeler. And there was this odd taste in his mouth, as if he'd been chewing on old sweat socks that had long since been forgotten in the bottom of a laundry hamper.

The smell of coffee and spring persisted. He saw no reason for either. If anything, his room should have smelled like a compost heap.

His eyes drifted over to the corner, where his wastepaper basket should have been. It was there, all right, but completely unencumbered by diapers.

Hadn't he...?

It slowly penetrated his mind that the room was neat. All of it. There was no container of overturned talcum, no used diapers waiting for further disposal, no hint of chaos of any kind.

It was even neater than he normally kept it. The blanket he'd used to separate his bedspread from Rachel's overactive bottom was neatly folded at the foot of his bed. Even the pile of empty diaper boxes had gone the way of the used diapers and disappeared.

Evan looked around again, completely confused. Maybe he had dreamed it after all.

Uncertain about the stability of his mind, he walked cautiously to the closed door.

As soon as he opened it, he heard Libby announce, "He's up!" and knew that if this was a bad dream, he was still trapped inside it.

Before he could say a word, Libby grabbed him by the hand. She immediately commenced chattering like one of the scrub jays that appeared by his window in the early spring. It seemed that her enforced silence had only given her that much more energy to exude on him, now that he was awake.

"Mama's got coffee for you." With the guileless determination of a terrier puppy, Libby began tugging him toward the kitchen. "She said to tell her as soon as you were awake, but not to wake you." She smiled up at him brightly. "So I didn't. Mama says that's what makes me a big girl. Do you think I'm a big girl?"

Evan's head was swimming. He was vaguely aware that Libby was asking him questions, but he couldn't quite make out what they were. The only thing his brain had latched onto was the word *coffee,* and it was hanging on to it as if it were a life preserver.

Maybe coffee would help him make sense of what was going on. He stumbled the rest of the way to the kitchen, still in Libby's wake.

Coffee was waiting for him at the table. Yes, there was still some order to the universe.

Evan automatically picked up the cup in both hands and drank, then swore, breaking the word off in the middle when he realized that Libby was still standing there.

"Careful, it's hot," Claire warned needlessly after the fact, then shook her head. "But you already know that."

Nursing his bottom lip, Evan sipped the rest of the coffee slowly, needing the liquid and what it could do for him more than he needed to keep himself from getting burned. When he finished, he set the cup down and looked around, getting his bearings.

He knew for a fact that he'd left the kitchen in an advanced state of upheaval, trying to warm bottles for Rachel while keeping her from wailing. Yet everything was washed and replaced, as if he'd never even been in here last night. No spilled mess, no pots flung every which way, no empty milk carton left standing. It hardly looked like his kitchen.

She'd worked nothing short of a miracle, he thought as he slowly began to feel like his old self again. Evan looked around a second time. He'd always admired the ability to organize. Last night, he'd thought that he had completely lost the knack himself, utterly undone by a six-month-old.

He turned to look at Claire. She was by the stove, busy with something that was sizzling. "Do you hire out?" he asked, only half joking.

She looked at him over her shoulder, a smile dazzling him. "You couldn't afford me."

"Probably not." As consciousness settled in to stay, so did the grudging admiration. Grudging because she'd succeeded where he had obviously failed. "How did you manage?"

It wasn't in her nature to brag, although this time she was a little tempted.

"I've had more on-the-job training than you," she replied simply. With Rachel nestled comfortably against one hip, Claire crossed to the table and poured Evan a second cup of coffee. "Try not to burn your mouth this time."

He began to protest that he'd been half-asleep, then gave it up. Life-reaffirming coffee was more important than his pride.

Setting the pot down, Claire surprised him by cupping his chin in her hand before he had the opportunity to bring the second serving to his lips. She examined his mouth.

"Doesn't look too bad." She smiled into his eyes. "You'll be yelling again in no time."

Yelling was the farthest thing from his mind at the moment. What was on his mind was that he was very, very conscious of the touch of her hand, the feel of her skin against his.

And the lack of it when she drew her hand away and picked up the coffeepot again.

He couldn't seem to clear the fog from his brain, he

thought, not quite sure if it was Rachel, his sleepless night or Claire who was responsible. Probably a combination of all three. He grasped at straws, trying to draw her attention away from the fact that she left him tongue-tied.

"Um," he began, looking around again, "you didn't have to do this."

Thank you would have been nice, she thought, but she shrugged in reply.

"I drink coffee, too. And eat." Deftly, using only one hand, she shifted the contents of the frying pan to a plate and then brought it over to the table. "Libby and I helped ourselves to some toast and juice."

Claire set down the omelet she'd prepared for him out of odds and ends she'd found in the refrigerator. It was obvious that he either didn't believe in eating at home a great deal, or had takeout sent in most of the time. There had been almost nothing to work with.

Deciding she needed a break, Claire went to the living room to place Rachel in the swing.

Maybe it was magic, he thought, looking at the omelet. He couldn't remember the last time he'd had a home-cooked meal, other than at his mother's house.

"I didn't mean just the coffee," he told her. "Or break-fast."

"What?" she called from the other room. "I can't hear you."

"I said," he began, his voice raised, only to realize that she'd returned, "I didn't mean just the coffee or the break-fast." He looked at her empty arms. "Where's the baby?"

"I put her in the swing." She nodded toward the living room. "Libby's watching her. They seem to have taken a shine to each other." There was pure affection in her smile. "I guess it's good for Libby not to be the center of the universe for a while."

Claire sat down at the table, shifting her chair so that she could keep an eye on her daughter and Rachel, just in case. Libby might be growing up, but she was far from grown.

For the moment, though, Evan had her attention. She liked him better this way, she decided, messy, with the residue of sleep in his eyes.

"That's a good sign, you know. Your asking about the baby, I mean. I guess I might have misjudged you."

He raised his eyes to hers and she explained.

"You have potential to be a good father."

She was giving him credit where none was due. And he was still a long way off from declaring himself Rachel's father. "Look, I'm just trying to do the right thing and take care of her for a few days—just until I find out what's going on."

Maybe she hadn't misjudged him all that much, Claire thought, drawing back. Maybe she was just being too lenient because there was something about him that transcended their obviously different points of view. Something that silently reached out to her.

She had to stop trying to be everyone's mother, she reminded herself.

Claire pinned him with a long, scrutinizing look. "You're still sticking to your story that she's not yours?"

He didn't like the way she worded that. "It's not a story. It's the truth." And then, as before, uncertainty nibbled at his denial, making him waver. He didn't believe in lying. "At least, I think so." He clung to what he knew for certain. "I never saw her before the day before yesterday. Some woman left her with my secretary, saying it—she—was mine."

The intensity of his words convinced her he was telling the truth, no matter what it sounded like. Claire arched an eyebrow. "Women do this often with you?"

He couldn't tell whether or not she believed him and

didn't know why it was so important to him that she did. But for some reason, it was. "No, not often. This is a first."

"And you really have no idea...?" Claire's voice trailed off.

Did she think he was some kind of promiscuous womanizer who bedded women solely for the satisfaction of having done it? Women weren't trophies to him; they were alien creatures he didn't have a prayer of understanding. Present company included.

"Of course I have an idea. A vague one," he amended after a beat. "I'm not exactly the village seducer." He looked at his cup. It was empty. He needed more to fortify himself against her. Evan turned his attention to his breakfast. "That's more my brother's line."

Claire glanced toward the living room. Libby was busy kissing Rachel's feet each time the swing went forward. Rachel seemed to like it. She had a few more minutes of respite.

"There are more like you?"

He thought of Devin. "I wouldn't say he was more like me. He's my twin brother, but we're not alike. We're not alike at all."

So Evan had a twin, too. At least he knew where his twin was, she thought ruefully. Until her father's friend had made that slip last week, she hadn't even known she had a twin. And she certainly didn't know where to start looking for her.

"You mean he's friendly?" The sharp look Evan gave her had Claire raising her hands in surrender. "Sorry, maybe that was a little low, but you do have to admit, you bite people's heads off." In a vague way, he reminded her of her father. There was that same tendency to keep her at arm's length. "If you were a doctor, your bedside manner would be classified as lousy."

"Well, I'm not a doctor." He finished eating and pushed

back the plate just as his appetite vanished. "What I am, though, is very busy and I don't have any time for this—"

Oh, no, not this refrain again. She'd already given him points for getting past it. She really was too soft on people, she thought. Just because he looked like a rumpled puppy dog didn't make him one.

"You took some time off, remember? A week's vacation. Your secretary arranged it."

The true meaning of her words sank in, possibly for the first time. "A week of this?" He looked like a man who had just heard his death sentence.

Despite her best intentions to the contrary, Claire couldn't help softening again. She laughed at the hapless expression on his face.

"It gets better." She rose, clearing away his plate. "Speaking of which, do you feel any better? You slept like a dead man."

He wanted to say no, he didn't feel any better, but that would be a lie.

"Yeah, some." He caught a whiff of her fragrance, and it brought an instant reaction. Springtime. "Did you come into my room while I was asleep?" Or had that just been unconscious wishful thinking on his part?

"Just to clean up." She'd left his bedroom to the very end, thinking he might wake up first. When he didn't, she'd parked Rachel in her crib and gone in, restoring order as quickly as she could. She didn't care for cleaning, but she was good at it when she set her mind to it. "I didn't think the pile of diapers you left there would have been the most aesthetic thing for you to wake up to."

No, but she would be. The thought sneaked up on him, taking him completely by surprise, as Evan watched Claire move more effortlessly through his kitchen than he did. As if she belonged there.

He had the feeling that she could make herself at home anywhere.

"Thanks." The word seemed hopelessly inadequate for everything she'd done, but while he had the ability to compose twenty-page memos on the spot with absolutely no effort at all, once the matter was personal, his ready supply of words seemed to all but dry up.

"Don't mention it." The moment hung awkwardly between them. She did her best to brush it away. "So," Claire continued, trying to sound as if she was making casual conversation, "you think you might know who Rachel's mother is?" She turned on the water and began scrubbing the frying pan furiously to hide an uncustomary onslaught of nerves.

He had his suspicions. Actually, he doubted it could be anyone else. *If* this baby actually was his. "Devin's looking into it for me."

"Devin?" She set the pan on the rack and turned around.

"My brother. He's a private investigator." Evan was more surprised than she must be to hear himself telling her any of this. He didn't usually trot out his family for people.

Claire cocked her head, studying him. She tried to picture him and his brother together and couldn't quite manage it. "No kidding. He really *is* different from you, isn't he?"

Evan laughed dryly. He'd heard that often enough. "Like night and day." Devin was day, while he was night. Women generally preferred the day.

Differences were what made things interesting. She wondered if his brother lived anywhere close.

"It must have been nice, though, having someone to talk to when you were growing up." She'd spent her entire childhood wishing she'd had a brother or sister to share the loneliness with. It hurt horribly to discover that she had had one all along without knowing it, without being able to do anything about finding her. "I imagine you must have been close at one point." She finished washing off his plate and set it next to the pan to dry.

Evan considered for a minute. "Maybe. I was closer to one of my sisters, really."

"Sisters?" She dried her hands and draped the towel over the back of the chair before sitting down again. "How many are there in your family?"

She sounded as if she was really interested, he thought, and wondered why. "Four, counting me, not counting my parents. How many in yours?"

The question seemed to come of its own accord. As a rule, he didn't delve into people's private lives. He simply had no curiosity about others to prompt the questions, not the way Devin had.

But Claire was different. She made him curious. Maybe because the circumstances he found himself in with her were so unusual.

"Two," she said firmly. "Libby and me."

He had the strangest feeling a door had just shut. "I meant—"

"I know what you meant," she said tersely. The rest came out as if she were reciting it. "I was an only child." There was no point in telling him about the sister she'd never known. "My mother died when I was six. My father was a surgeon. I hardly ever saw him."

He picked up on the crucial word. "'Was'?"

"Was," she repeated. "He died, too, before Libby was born."

She had no grandfather to give her daughter, and no grandmother. That bothered her at times, although it didn't seem to faze Libby any more than not having a father did. She was one terrific little girl, Claire thought warmly.

"So," Claire concluded briskly, "in a way, that makes her my whole family."

There was more here, he thought, deciding to turn the tables on her and press. "'In a way'?"

She shrugged, looking off. There was no reason this should make her uncomfortable, except, perhaps, in the manner it had been revealed to her. Like some dark secret to be atoned for. But then, that had been her father's doing.

"I was adopted," she said matter-of-factly. "Maybe that's why I relate so much to Rachel. We were both given away." She realized that there was more emotion in her voice than she had intended and was quick to remedy that. "My birth mother gave me away, and my adoptive father couldn't find it in his heart to get close to me."

The smile on her face was sad, Evan thought. It stirred something within him, a desire to comfort, to protect. It was, he realized, a first for him. He rather liked it, although for the time being, he didn't explore why. Life was complicated enough for him right now as it was.

"When I was little, I used to think it was because of something I had done. Oh, he was a nice man and all that," Claire added quickly. "I had all the creature comforts a kid could want. Except for love." And without love, she thought, none of the rest had really meant anything. "He just couldn't find it in his heart to love a stranger. That was the way he always thought of me, he said, as a stranger. I didn't know that until he was dying. He made a confession to me. A dramatic deathbed scene during which he asked my forgiveness."

She pressed her lips together. It seemed foolish to let this hurt now. It was years in the past. But it made no difference. She had had so much love to give her father, and he'd never wanted it. It had all gone to waste.

"It seemed that he'd never wanted to adopt me. It was all his wife's idea. And then she died and left him to take care of me. Poor man, he was never cut out to be a father. He had a lousy bedside manner, too."

A sad smile turned to one of compassion as she thought of Douglas Walker. It hadn't been his fault, either. He just didn't have it in him to love anyone other than his wife.

"He was a really great neurosurgeon, but not a man to shoot the breeze with. Or derive any comfort from."

"And you forgave him?"

"Sure. What else could I do? Besides, I was so relieved that it wasn't because of anything I had done."

Another woman, he thought, would have withheld forgiveness, feeling that revenge was her due.

Claire blew out a breath. She'd talked way too much. "All right, there you have it, my life story."

"Not quite." Evan looked toward the living room. She knew he was thinking of Libby.

"We'll save that for another time." With an air of finality, Claire rose and pushed her chair against the table. "All right, if you're sufficiently fed and rested, Libby and I have to be going."

The thought of her leaving didn't rest any better with him now than it did last night.

"Um, look, I have to check in with my office. Not physically, just over the telephone," he explained quickly before she could get it into her head to deliver another lecture, or worse, just turn on her heel and leave. He put himself on the line and asked, "Could you hang around until I finish?"

She felt uncomfortable after what she'd just told him. There was no reason for her to have said all that she had. It wasn't as if she'd been reacting to his compassion or sympathy. If anything, she'd been reacting to Rachel's dilemma.

Right now, all she wanted to do was go home. "How long a conversation?"

He wasn't about to give her an exact time frame. This way, if he ran over, she'd still stay.

"Not long."

There was nothing pressing for her to do now that she had fed Libby. She was still running on empty as far as work went, and staring at the blank screen would only depress her.

"All right, I guess I can manage that. Go ahead, make your call. And while you're at it," she added just as he began to leave, "squeeze in a shower and change your clothes."

She was being gracious again. Evan looked down. Accustomed to always being impeccably dressed, he knew he should feel self-conscious, but for some reason, he didn't. Not around her. He wondered what that meant. "I guess I do look pretty awful."

Claire smiled. "Not awful, just wrinkled and stained." She smoothed out his shirt collar, but it was hopeless at this point. The whole shirt needed to be cleaned and pressed. "I'll see if I can get some of this out for you."

He placed his hand over hers to stop her fingers from fluttering and from causing his breakfast to churn in a stomach suddenly gone tight. He was going to tell her that she didn't have to, then stopped himself when he realized that he wanted her to.

"I'd appreciate that." The words dripped from his lips, his eyes on hers.

He wasn't finished; she could tell by the way he left the end hanging. "And?" she prodded, waiting.

Something had been bothering him all the time she'd been sitting across from him. All the time he'd been looking at her. Unfinished business.

"And, I'd like to kiss you again. This time, not by accident."

Claire felt her pulse jump. It always did when she was asking for trouble. And this was probably a double helping. The smart thing would be just to walk away. Quickly.

It was a hard thing to admit about herself, but she wasn't always smart.

"All right." Her hand brushed against his collar, threading along the back of his neck. "Will that be with or without starch?"

"Without," he answered as he lowered his mouth to hers.

Chapter Seven

It wouldn't have been easy for Evan to put what he was experiencing into words. It didn't matter. Whatever words he would have used wouldn't have been sufficient. Wouldn't have begun to describe what was really happening.

Except, perhaps, the word *more*.

For kissing Claire was more than anything he'd ever experienced. Sweeter, sexier, more exciting, more seductive.

More.

So much more that it left Evan in awe. How could something as simple as a kiss make him momentarily forget everything else? His surroundings, his dilemma, the fact that the last thing in the world he needed right now was to become entangled with another woman. After all, if that little bundle from heaven really did turn out to be his, there would be her mother to deal with. There was a moral responsibility Evan meant to face up to. One that any lawyer he might have engaged would have cringed at. But Evan didn't believe in shunning his obligations. If Rachel was his, he meant to take care of her and her mother financially.

That didn't change what was going on now.

He was entangled. From that moment on, whether he liked it or not, Evan Quartermain knew that he had come face-to-face with his undoing and it stood about five foot three. He sensed it the way a parachutist sensed the thrill of his first jump a moment before he leaped from the airplane.

Evan jumped. There really was little else he could do. He wound his arms around Claire, pressing her to him, and he jumped. Right into the heart of the kiss. Right into no-man's-land.

And lost himself in her.

He deepened the kiss, savoring her taste, her scent, the feel of her body against his, and embraced his undoing.

The room was spinning around Claire. Shaking? San Francisco had never fully breathed a sigh of relief since the last earthquake and always slept with one eye opened. Was this another earthquake? she wondered.

It surely felt like one. If not one of the land, then of the soul. Rather than run for a door frame for shelter, Claire clung to the only thing that gave her stability.

The origin of the quake itself.

Like a blind person trying to see, Claire slipped her hands along Evan's face, committing everything to memory within her mind's eye. She wound her fingers into his thick dark hair and gloried in the way his body pressed against hers.

This was what that faint brush of lips had hinted at. Passion and fire, comfort and disquietude. In short, a one-stop haven for everything.

Somewhere, from a galaxy far, far away, a small voice called to her. "Mama, Rachel's hungry."

Rachel wasn't the only one, Evan thought, dazed. Libby's urgent call succeeded in peeling them apart. Shaken, stunned, Evan drew back, too numbed to say anything at first. All he could do was look at Claire in abject wonder. She was attractive—he'd been aware of that from the beginning—with straight, long blond hair, a tidy, athletic body that would have set any man's mind wandering and legs that would make his mouth water. But there was no way he would have thought she packed such a wallop.

His stomach still felt as if it was quaking.

All systems were not go. Claire could have sworn she felt her blood scrambling in her veins, running for high ground against the flood of feelings Evan's kiss had let loose. Feelings she had to rein in before they threatened to make a complete mess of the life she had so carefully constructed for herself and Libby.

She didn't want to pull at the reins; she wanted to feel, and that was the very real problem.

"Maybe I'd better go feed her," Claire mumbled. She backed away from him and out of the room with as much grace as she could muster, given the circumstances.

He nodded as feeling returned to his limbs. "Maybe you'd better."

And maybe, Evan thought as he watched her walk quickly into the next room, he had better take another shower. A much colder one than the one he'd taken earlier.

Hands wrapped around the doorjamb, her feet pressed tightly to one side against the corner, Libby swung to and fro, watching her mother work. Impatience was written all over her fair face.

"Isn't it time *yet*, Mama?" She'd been popping into Claire's office, asking the same question every few minutes for the past two hours.

Tenaciously hanging on to her train of thought, Claire looked up from the screen. For the first time since Evan Quartermain and the baby he refused to refer to as his daughter had entered her life a week ago, she was actually making headway on the presentation she was supposed to have been working on since the beginning of the month. The deadline was next week. Appropriately enough, she was to hand it in just before Thanksgiving. If Aesthetic Athletics, a company that manufactured everything from running shoes to major gym equipment, liked what she put together for them, they were going to put her on their payroll. That would be something to really be thankful for.

Claire liked freelancing, but there was something to be said for steady money and Aesthetic Athletics had a great deal of it. It would mean a lot to her and Libby as far as stability went.

So she really wasn't in the mood for interruptions, especially when those interruptions had anything to do with Evan Quartermain.

Damn it, she couldn't even think of his name without feeling a tiny tremor rippling through her. Which was just the trouble. She didn't need or want tremors, tiny or otherwise, rippling through her. Ever since he'd shaken up her life, she'd done her best to maintain a polite, helpful but definite distance from him.

It hadn't been easy, especially since for the first few days of his "forced vacation"—as he referred to the time off he'd taken—he had been on the telephone to her on the average of once every seventy minutes, asking for advice, asking for help or just plain asking. It was a matter, she understood, of trying to keep his sanity when confronted with a completely unfamiliar set of circumstances. Just because he'd made it through one night didn't make him a veteran, or even ensure that he could get through another night intact.

She sympathized, but she left her barriers up.

True to her word, Claire had responded to each and every call, giving him advice, support and assurance. Most of the time, she wound up coming over to help in person rather than coaching over the phone. It was easier that way, at least as far as helping to care for Rachel went. Claire had the consolation of knowing that even if *she* was uncomfortable, Libby loved it.

And, she had to admit, caring for Rachel was a joy. She loved holding a sweet, cuddly baby in her arms. But it was also a problem. The problem was that she knew she was getting much too close to a child she had no business having feelings for.

At the very best, this was all just temporary. Once Evan's brother located Rachel's mother, one of any number of things could happen. And Claire didn't figure into any of the solutions. She would be left on the outside, missing a baby who wasn't hers.

But it was hard not melting at the sight of a smile that lit up a room. And by now, Rachel recognized her; Claire was sure of it. The baby extended her arms to her whenever Claire entered the room. Once or twice would have been a coincidence. Several times was not. Rachel knew her, responded to her. It would have taken an iron heart to remain under wraps.

And Claire's heart was definitely not made of iron.

Being around Evan proved that to her. Despite her best intentions, Claire could feel herself tingle whenever he entered a room, her body bracing for what she knew she shouldn't want, shouldn't have.

For what she desperately desired.

She wanted him to kiss her again. To have him hold her as if she were something precious.

Looking back, Claire knew that she had merely fooled herself into thinking she no longer wanted that kind of affection. The funny thing was, she had actually believed she didn't need it. Until she had come face-to-face with it again. Now she knew that she'd only been trying to sell herself a tissue of lies.

Though she adored Libby and loved her work, there was still a part of Claire that was empty, a part of her that felt needy. That same part that had never really been filled. She'd once thought that she'd found her answer in Jack—she'd believed that his love would make up for the emptiness she had endured all her young life.

But what she'd thought was love had turned out to be something less, something as disposable as the diapers she'd once used for Libby. It wasn't meant to endure, or to fulfill.

And neither, she upbraided herself now, was what she felt, or thought she felt, when Evan kissed her. It was a fluke, nothing more. She'd overreacted because she hadn't been with a man in any sort of intimate fashion since Jack had walked out on her. Hell, she hadn't been with a man without her graphic-arts portfolio between them in years. But that was her choice, and intellectually, it was a good one.

Her body had other ideas, but her body, Claire thought ruefully, had been her undoing before. She didn't want to be undone again. This time, she knew, she might not be able to glue back the pieces into any sort of working order.

Besides, Evan obviously wasn't interested in her in any other capacity than that of an impromptu nanny for his baby, or whatever it was he preferred to think of Rachel as being. If he were the least bit interested, he would have tried to kiss her again. Would have at least picked up on the fact that she *wanted* to be kissed again. Men were supposed to have radar about things like that.

But Evan Quartermain, damn him, had made no moves whatsoever in that direction.

Which was, she told herself, actually a very good thing, given the nature of her vulnerability. Getting involved with him wouldn't be a smart thing to do. The situation was far too complicated for her to just walk into. Evan had a baby and a responsibility to that baby's mother, wherever and whoever she was. There was no place for Claire in that kind of equation. Whatever else she might be, she knew she wasn't the other-woman type.

It was better this way for her. A lot better.

Claire punched a key on the keyboard. If it was so much better, why did she feel so damn restless?

"Mama, are you listening to me?"

No longer in the doorway, her daughter was now hanging off the back of her swivel chair. Very carefully, Claire pried off ten little fingers.

"All the time, honey."

Libby fisted her hands at her waist and fixed her with a look Claire knew the little girl had been on the receiving end of more than once. It wasn't easy to keep from laughing, but somehow, she managed.

"Then what did I say?" Libby demanded. It was obvious she had her doubts about her mother's statement.

Claire folded her hands in her lap and did her best to look contrite. "You asked if it was time yet."

The little face unclouded. Mama was listening after all. "Okay." The word absolved her mother of any blame. "So, is it?"

Claire sighed. The last thing she wanted was to go over there now. She didn't need him distracting her, and for once, the phone calls hadn't been coming with the regularity of a pendulum marking time.

"No, it's not."

Libby refused to give in so easily this time. "But maybe he needs us."

"Then he'll call," Claire assured her. She returned to the logo she was creating. "He's been calling all the time."

Libby pushed herself into her mother's line of vision. "But not today. Maybe something's wrong." She chewed on her lip, concerned. It wasn't so much Mr. Q. she was thinking of, but Rachel. "She's awfully little, Mama," she declared as if it were news. "What if he did something to her, something wrong, and doesn't know how to undo it now?"

The child had much too much imagination. That, Claire knew, was something she'd inherited from her.

"Nothing's wrong, Libby," Claire told her soothingly. "He's just getting better at taking care of Rachel, that's all. Even monkeys learn if you train them."

Or maybe he was celebrating his pending return to work, she added silently. Evan had lined up a nanny who was to begin on Monday, which, Claire knew, he was looking upon as his independence day. He was returning to work, and life was returning to normal.

There would be no need for her shortly. Maybe even now, she thought ruefully. Just as well. Claire stabbed at another key, almost breaking a nail.

Libby tugged on the chair, bringing it around to face her. Huge blue eyes plaintively looked up at her mother. "Please, Mama? For me? Can we go over and check?"

Claire sighed. A few keystrokes shut down the computer, and she rose, pushing back her chair. She really had to get better at saying no to Libby.

Maybe tomorrow.

She wondered if Libby knew the kind of power she wielded over her. Probably. "Okay, just this once."

Libby was out of the room before she finished. Claire heard the front door opening.

"Libby, wait for me," she called, even though she knew it was useless. The girl was like a bullet when presented with a target.

Making sure she had her keys, Claire hurried after her daughter. She reached Evan's front door a full minute after Libby. Standing on her toes for added leverage, Libby was leaning on the doorbell.

If Rachel was sleeping, she was awake now, Claire

thought guiltily as she removed Libby's finger from the bell. Just as she did, the front door opened.

Claire avoided his eyes. "I'm sorry," she apologized, struggling not to flush like a teenager urged on by her girl-friends to ring the school hunk's doorbell. "This was Libby's idea," she hurried to explain, looking down at her daughter. She was holding on to Libby to keep her from dashing inside. "She got worried when you didn't call to-day and thought you might need help. I told her you were probably just getting better at taking care of Rachel."

Claire finally had enough courage to look at him, afraid of seeing amusement in his face. There was no amusement. There was sweat, and flushed cheeks that conflicted with the rest of his pasty pallor. His eyes were one step away from glassy.

It took her a minute to find her tongue. "You look aw-ful."

Though he knew he did, Evan's first thought was to deny it. Masculine pride prevented him from admitting that he felt as weak as a kitten being blown around in a gale.

"Are you all right?" Claire asked before he could force the denial out of his mouth. She touched his forehead. "No," she answered her own question, "you are definitely not all right. Evan, you're burning up." Not waiting for an invitation, she came in, instantly taking charge. "Why didn't you call me?"

Claire looked around for Rachel. The baby wasn't any-where in the living room.

He'd been battling this feeling since late last night, and it was becoming increasingly difficult to focus his mind or his eyes. Both were becoming watery. "I didn't want to seem like a wimp."

The answer stunned her. "Because you're sick? That's stupid."

The word penetrated the fog that was closing in on his

brain. Stupid. That was him, all right. Not like Devin. Devin was smart. Devin had it all. Admiration, time to breathe. Everything.

"I didn't want to look stupid, either," he mumbled into his chin.

He really was out of it, she thought. "Well, you failed. You need to get into bed."

It took him a minute to absorb what she was telling him. Then he shook his head and nearly keeled over. He steadied himself by grabbing on to her shoulder.

"Can't. I've got a baby to take care of. Rachel, remember?"

She braced her legs to keep from falling. Evan was leaning more than a little of his weight on her. "I've been here most of the time—it's a little hard to forget."

If she lived forever, she was never going to understand the way a man's mind worked. He'd called her for everything from what temperature a bottle should be to whether or not it was all right to use packing tape to hold a diaper together if the tabs broke, which they seemed to do for him with a fair amount of regularity. He called her with questions she knew he knew the answers to. And yet when he really should have called her, asking for help, he didn't. Why?

Libby stared in fascination at the way perspiration was beading along Evan's forehead. There was triumph in her face. "See, Mama, see? I told you something was wrong."

"Yes, you did, Libby."

He was going to fall flat on his face any minute, Claire thought in horror. In an effort to steady him, she took his arm and laid it across her shoulders. She didn't want Libby underfoot right now.

"Go check on Rachel for me, honey." Just as she thought, he was beginning to sink. Claire did her best to keep him upright. "I'm going to get Mr. Quartermain to bed."

His head was really swimming now, and incoherent thoughts were slipping in and out of his brain like minnows in a pond. Had she just propositioned him? It certainly sounded that way. Why did she have to do it now, when he had no strength?

"Shh." He tried to lay a finger to his lips and missed. "Not in front of your daughter."

Astonishment gave way to laughter. Claire shook her head, then braced her arm around his back as he began to sink again. "I think you're getting delirious, Mr. Quartermain."

"Naw." He shook his head and instantly regretted it. "My head's as clear as a bell. You want me in bed. I want you in bed. See?" He looked at her and was surprised to find how close her face was to his. Had she been standing here all along? "Clear."

Libby, poised to run off, stopped and regarded Evan curiously. "Does he think you're sick, too, Mama? Are you? Your cheeks are pink, like his."

She didn't doubt it. Though she believed in being truthful with Libby, this was a little too delicate to go into right now. "I'm just struggling, honey. He's very heavy. Now scoot, Libby. Do as I told you." Libby was gone in a flash, rushing off to Rachel's room. "C'mon, macho man, I'll get you to bed."

When he began to weave, Claire was quick to compensate for the motion and managed to keep both of them from falling over. Very carefully, she led him to the stairs and tried not to think how many there were.

Evan sighed deeply. "Strong," was his only comment. And then he shuddered.

He was burning up. She had to get him to bed before he collapsed. There was no way she would be able to get him off the floor. Struggling, she had visions of both of them toppling down the stairs.

"But not an Olympic contender, so you're going to have to help me here." She was already sinking under the added weight. The man's arm seemed to be getting heavier with each step she took. "One foot in front of the other, Mr. Quartermain."

He did as he was told, his mind drifting farther and farther away from him.

"Stop calling me that," he muttered. "Like my teachers. They always called me Mr. Quartermain. You're not my teacher." He turned his head to look at her and swayed. Claire yelped as she caught hold of his shirt. "Are you?"

"No, I'm still feeling my way around, learning, just like you, Evan," she murmured. They were nearly at his door and it was none too soon for her. There was almost as much perspiration on her forehead as there was on his.

"Good. Evan's good." As he drew a breath, his head filled with her scent. Good enough to eat, he thought. He grinned foolishly at her. "Wanna play hooky together?"

If he remembered any of this tomorrow, he was going to feel like an idiot, she thought. Life had its little compensations.

"You really *are* out of it, aren't you?" She tightened her hold on the hand that was slung over her shoulder and took smaller steps, afraid of losing him. "I've got to hand it to Libby, she got me here just in time." She spoke slower as his weight robbed her lungs of air. "She thought there was something wrong when you didn't call. I just thought you were getting better at it."

"Nope. Not better. Worse." He sighed the word. "All I think about is you."

He'd misunderstood her meaning. The right thing would have been to stop him right there, before he told her anything else he would rather she didn't know. But she wouldn't have been human if she didn't want to hear more. Claire let him go on talking.

It was probably only the ramblings of a delirious man, she told herself. But still…

"You do, huh?"

"Yeah." He was slipping again, and she struggled to keep him from sinking all the way, half dragging him now toward his bed. "How I'd like to kiss you again. How I'd like to undress you, slow, and watch your eyes when I touch you."

Whether he was delirious or not, his words were creating images for her. Images that made her warmer than he was right now. Her heart began hammering erratically, and she knew her uphill struggle with him was only partially to blame.

"Right now, I'd suggest you just watch your step." *Almost there,* she thought, eyeing his bed. *Almost there.*

"That's the trouble. I have been. All my life," he mourned. "And where did it get me?"

"I don't know. A nice house?" When had his room become so big? And why was his bed so far from the damn door?

"Sure, a great house. And a better career than Devin's, with lots more money. But what good is that?" he demanded suddenly with feeling, before adding sadly, "I'm alone."

He didn't mean this, she thought. Not any of it. That was just the fever talking. She couldn't take him seriously. She couldn't afford to.

"You're not alone," she argued. "You have Rachel."

"Rachel." He said the name as if thinking about the child. "I don't know if I have Rachel. She might not be mine. Maybe it's a mistake. All a mistake." And then he shifted again. Claire stumbled at the foot of his bed. She threw rather than guided him down onto his bed, face first.

"But I'd rather have you." His words were muffled against the bedspread.

He was going to suffocate if she left him that way, she thought. Claire took hold of his shoulder and tried to pull him around. "You don't know what you're saying." With one mighty tug, she succeeded in getting him onto his back. "And I'm talking to an unconscious man."

Evan was sound asleep.

Chapter Eight

Evan had the sensation that he was floating over a river of lava.

Incredible, insurmountable heat surrounded him, obscuring everything so that he couldn't see. He didn't know where he was, only that he was lost and that it was hot.

The heat made him feel as if he were unraveling and growing progressively weaker. There wasn't enough strength to lift his head or move his limbs. He wasn't even sure if he had any limbs.

He couldn't feel them, couldn't feel anything, only the heat.

And then, through the vapors, there was the sensation that someone was holding him. Someone was lifting his head and touching something to his lips. It was cool and slipped down his throat and along his mouth. A little trickled down his chin.

He thought he might have swallowed, but he wasn't sure.

Evan faded again, never quite surfacing, never quite managing to break through the smothering blanket that kept him down.

The dollop of coolness returned and then spread. This time, he felt it along his forehead and on his hands. No, on his wrists. Like bracelets. With it came a sensation of wetness, a circle of cold wetness around each wrist.

Wetness.

Rachel?

Where was Rachel? He had to take care of Rachel. Panic pierced him. He'd left her alone. He had to get back to her. She needed him.

"Rachel."

He said her name aloud. It took the last bit of strength he had, but he knew he forced her name past his lips. Someone had to hear him; someone had to help.

Someone.

Claire.

Claire could help. She had to help.

"Claire." He whispered her name like a prayer.

There was a pressure on his chest, forcing him down. Had he been trying to get up? He didn't know, didn't know anything. Except that he had to find Rachel and only Claire could help.

And then he sank back into nothingness, letting it swallow him up. He was too weak to struggle against it.

Evan slowly opened his eyes. They felt hot and itchy. And heavy. It took him several tries before they would remain open. And then it took him more time to focus and orient himself.

He was in his room. It was gloomy, but there was no light on. Was it morning? There was a light, rhythmic tapping sound against his window. Rain. It was daytime and it was raining.

He didn't remember getting into bed, but he must have. How else could he have gotten here?

And then he saw her. Claire. Sitting in a chair near his bed, her eyes shut. She looked as if she was dozing.

This wasn't real. He had to be dreaming. But it felt real. As real as the ache in his head.

What was she doing here like this?

Evan tried to sit up. A groan twisted from his lips. The very act of propping himself up on his elbows sapped all the available strength from his body like the last bit of liquid being sipped through a straw.

His groan woke her. Claire was on her feet instantly, crossing to him. The concern that furrowed her brow faded when she saw that his eyes were open and no longer glassy. They were focused on her.

Her smile was accompanied by a sigh of relief. He'd had her worried, even after the doctor had assured her he'd be all right.

"Hi." She banked down the desire to feather her fingers through his hair. "Welcome back."

Back? Had he been somewhere? Evan tried to think, but his head felt like a vacuum. A large, throbbing vacuum.

"What are you doing here?" Each word seemed to stick to his lips. They felt like dried sandpaper, and his voice sounded incredibly hoarse to his ears.

Claire moved her shoulders, trying to work out the stiffness. She must have fallen asleep, she thought ruefully. It was rare that both children were down at the same time.

"Getting a crick in my neck." She rubbed it quickly, then bent over to touch her lips to his head in the age-old fashion of mothers everywhere. Satisfaction curved her mouth. "You're cooler. Finally."

Straightening, Claire blew out a breath. It had been a long two days, and she was beginning to think she was going to have to call Dr. Richmond for a return visit. Not that he would have minded. Sometimes it paid, she mused, to be the daughter of a doctor, even though she hadn't always thought so.

The fog in his brain refused to recede to shed any light on the situation. He was still unclear what she was doing here, although he vaguely remembered calling for her.

Or was that just a dream?

"I don't recall getting into bed."

Claire laughed, remembering. "There's a reason for that." She glanced at herself in the mirrored doors. She could stand a bit of tidying, she decided. All she could manage now was to run a hand through her hair. "You passed out before I could get you into it."

She got him into bed? When had that happened?

"And the pajamas?" he questioned. Raising the covers, Evan saw that he had on the bottoms, as well as the top. The last thing he remembered was that he was wearing clothes. And feeling like hell on a bad day.

Claire shrugged, purposely avoiding his eyes. She wasn't altogether sure what she'd see there or how she'd react to it. She was an adult, she'd done what she had to do and that was that.

That wasn't that. She'd undressed him and no matter what she told herself to the contrary, she *had* seen him naked. The man's clothes, impeccably tailored or not, hid a hell of a great body.

"Your clothes were soaked clean through." There wasn't a hint of emotion in her voice.

He still didn't quite believe what she had done. Had he missed something? When had they gotten on this footing?

"You undressed me?" There was a hint of a smile in his voice. And on his face when she looked.

Hers was the soul of innocence. "I'd rather think of it as dressing you in pajamas." And then she smiled. "Don't worry, I had my eyes shut the entire time."

"I wish I hadn't." He meant that sincerely.

There had been an intimacy between them, a moment when she had placed niceties aside and had thought only of caring for him.

And he had missed it completely by being out of his head when it had happened. There was no way to make up for that.

And then, suddenly, his thoughts went beyond his own needs, to someone whose needs were greater.

"Rachel—"

It pleased Claire to see the genuine concern on Evan's face. He wasn't just a caretaker anymore. The little girl was actually getting to mean something to him. There was hope for him yet.

"Don't worry, I've been looking after her. Libby's with her now. Last I checked, they were both sound asleep." She laughed softly, smoothing out the blankets and sheet he had tangled. "You're lucky Libby's too young to understand she could be charging you for baby-sitting. She's hardly left Rachel's side."

He could feel his energy trickling from him, like a tap that hadn't been properly closed. With a sigh, he lay back against his pillow, struggling to hold on to just a little of it.

Evan couldn't remember the last time he'd been sick. "How many hours have I been out of it?"

There was an odd smile on her face when she looked at him. He wondered what it meant.

"Try 'days.' "

For a moment, the word didn't fully register. "Days?"

She nodded. "Days." He really didn't realize how sick he was, did he? "It's Tuesday."

He'd been out only a few hours. Half a day, tops. She was pulling his leg. "That's impossible."

Claire wondered where Evan had gotten this idea that he

was nine parts invincible. "Want to see a newspaper?" she offered.

It wasn't that he didn't believe her; it was just that this new wrinkle made things so much more complicated. He'd just taken a week off to be with Rachel. He didn't have time to be sick, too.

"But I'm supposed to be at work."

"Surprise." He looked so befuddled, she took pity on him. Claire perched on the edge of the bed, taking his hand the way she would Libby's when she comforted her.

Maybe it would help him to know that things had been taken care of. "Don't worry, I called in and explained everything to Alma. Mr. Donovan said not to come back until you're well. He told me that he thought you'd work yourself into the ground someday."

She made it sound as if she and Donovan were old friends. Evan couldn't remember ever having a personal conversation with the man in all the years he'd been with the corporation. Despite the fact that Donovan had taken a liking to him, all they had ever talked about was work.

"You spoke to Donovan?"

Why did he look so surprised? she wondered. "He's a very nice man." Claire grinned, recalling the older man's words. "He said that he's happy you're in such 'capable hands.'"

Evan looked at the hand covering his. It looked too soft and delicate to be capable. But he was beginning to appreciate, firsthand, that she was. "Would you know if—?"

Claire could tell exactly what was on his mind. It wasn't difficult. "The takeover went through? No, it didn't."

She'd made a point of asking and writing down the answer Donovan gave her. The fact that she had asked had prompted Donovan's assessment of her. She decided not to mention that the man had said he'd looked forward to meeting her. That would put a definitely different spin on the relationship she and Evan had. She figured he didn't react well to that kind of pressure.

"The figures you came up with impressed the representatives of the Japanese corporation so much, they decided to invest in your company. Endicott's plans for a hostile takeover died a very grisly death, was the way Mr. Donovan saw it." She smiled, knowing Evan would be happy to hear this. "Seems you saved the day while lying flat on your back.

"Which is where you're going to stay for the rest of today and until you're feeling stronger," she added, negating any other ideas he might have.

That was fine with him. Right now, he had a feeling he couldn't get up even if he wanted to. But he did have a question.

Evan held up his wrists. "What are these? They look a little droopy for bondage."

A sense of humor, she thought. This was beginning to look promising. The next thing you knew, he would even be human.

"Compresses. Handkerchiefs, actually," Claire amended. "I improvised. Dr. Richmond thought they were a good idea when he came over."

Evan's eyebrows drew so close together, they formed one ripply dark line.

Maybe he was hallucinating again. Either that, or she was a witch. His vote was for the latter. Doctors never made house calls. "You had a doctor come over? How did you manage that?"

She decided that she liked catching him off guard like this. Liked the hint of admiration in his voice. She nodded. "Dr. David Richmond. He was my father's best friend. I got him to make a house call." Actually, it had just taken a phone call on her part. "I think he still feels guilty about his slip, so he came right over on his lunch hour."

"Slip? You mean as in malpractice?" Just what kind of a doctor had she called?

"No, as in slip of the tongue. He once told me something about myself he didn't realize I didn't know." A rueful smile quirked her lips. "Something my father neglected to tell me during his confession."

Evan waited, curious what sort of an unwitting revelation would make a doctor feel guilty.

She wasn't going to tell him, he realized, looking at her. His curiosity intensified. Evan wanted to know what sort of thing would upset her enough to make someone regret revealing it.

It was against his nature to pry. But then, it was also against his nature to be sick. "What did he tell you?"

She lifted a shoulder, then dropped it carelessly, as if she was trying to shrug off something. A weight, a feeling. Maybe she was.

Claire looked at Evan. He was a stranger. There was no reason to tell him anything.

Maybe there was no reason, but there was a need, she realized. A need to say it out loud and maybe make it finally disappear. It really wasn't anything of major consequence. Except to her.

And possibly to the sister she didn't know.

With a sigh, Claire looked out the window and watched the rain leave patterns on the pane. The way some things left patterns on the soul. Like tears.

"His exact words were, 'I wonder if your sister turned out as good as you did.'" She turned, looking at Evan pointedly. "I don't have a sister. I thought he had me confused with someone else and said so. Dr. Richmond looked very surprised. 'Didn't you know?' he asked. 'Your father told me he told you.'"

She knotted her fingers in her lap, something he noticed she did when she was feeling uncomfortable, defenseless.

"It seems that my father neglected to tell me everything. I had—have," she corrected, "a twin sister. My father didn't want to adopt any children—my mother wanted to adopt immediately. They compromised and took one baby. Me." She'd lost count of the number of times she'd wondered what life would have been like for her if they'd chosen the other baby. "When my mother finally talked him into taking in the second baby, as well, my sister had already been adopted. Of course, they were never told by who." Claire clenched her hands together in frustration. The same frustration she had felt in the past month, ever since she'd found out. "There's someone out there walking around with my face, and she probably doesn't know it."

Surprised at her own tone, she shrugged off the mood. "How did I get started talking about this?"

Evan had studied her face while she spoke. He didn't care for personal details. He saw them as needless, and they usually got in the way of things, of efficiency. But it was different with Claire.

He found himself wanting to know things about her. Little things, intimate things. For the first time in his life, he understood what motivated his brother's spark of curiosity.

"Dr. Richmond," he prompted gently.

"Right, Dr. Richmond." Feeling slightly embarrassed, Claire rose to her feet. She had to get back to the girls. Nap time was undoubtedly over. "Anyway, he came by, gave you a shot to lower your fever—it was pretty high by the time I called him." She'd debated calling an ambulance and decided to give the doctor a try first, knowing that Evan would have hated the fuss of being taken to the hospital emergency room. "And told me to watch you. So I did," she concluded brightly, trying to negate the somber moment she had just shared with him. "You didn't do any tricks."

Her playful tone didn't fool him. She had completely put

herself out for him without being asked. "You stayed here all that time?"

She wasn't quite sure if he would mind the invasion, but there was really no other choice. "Libby and I moved in. It seemed easier than dragging you over to my place." That had never even been a consideration. "You are one heavy man when you're limp."

Bits and pieces were coming back to him. He vaguely remembered the sound of her voice in his ear as he was stumbling up the stairs.

And there was more. "Wasn't the nanny supposed to start yesterday?"

He wasn't going to like this. "It's been postponed— indefinitely." She saw the confusion that creased his brow. "She wouldn't set one foot into the house when I said you were sick," Claire explained. "Didn't even let me explain. She was gone in a flash, saying you weren't paying her enough to risk getting sick. Personally, I didn't like her," Claire confided as she made her way to the door. "I think you should have been a little choosier."

She began to open the door, then remembered something else. So much had gone on while he was unconscious, it was hard to keep it all in order.

"Oh, and your brother called." She thought a moment, determined to get the message right. "He told me to tell you that he's still trying to locate Marilyn."

"Marilyn?" The name meant nothing to him. Should it? "Who's Marilyn?"

"Marilyn Schaffer." He still looked blank. Maybe his brain wasn't focusing yet. "That's what the cruise enter-tainer's name really was." She could see he still didn't understand. "Siren. Rachel's alleged mother?"

And then it dawned on him. The woman who had turned his life upside down. The woman whose face he barely remembered. The only woman whose face he could see clearly in his mind's eye was Claire.

"Oh."

The word gave her no clue. She wished she knew what he was thinking. Was he disappointed Devin couldn't find her, or relieved? And which did she want him to be?

It didn't matter what she wanted, she reminded herself. It was what was best for the baby that counted.

"Anyway, she quit her job. The cruise line's personnel director doesn't know where she went, and she moved out of the apartment she was leasing," Claire told him. "But Devin's got a list of people she knew and he's working on that." Finished with her recitation, she blew out a breath, then smiled. "He's got a nice voice."

Evan accepted the compliment for his brother with a nod, absently wondering if Devin had flirted with her. That he might have flirted stirred something within Evan that went beyond the rivalry he'd initiated between them so many years ago. There was an uneasiness he didn't quite understand.

"Some people say we sound alike on the phone." He dismissed the comment as petty. "Actually, they don't." Evan looked at Claire, at a loss. "You know, I don't know what to say."

Didn't he realize that she didn't want a profusion of words? That a simple thank-you would have been enough? And what was that comment about their voices all about? Was that a trace of jealousy? Claire shrugged; she'd probably just imagined it.

"Don't say anything, just go back to sleep," she instructed, then glanced at her watch. She'd dozed for only fifteen minutes. "The kids were both napping when I came in, and now that I know you're not going to slip into a coma, I'm going to get back to my own work."

Hesitating, Claire debated telling him, then decided she

should. He might find out anyway if Libby got into his room. So far, she'd impressed her daughter with the need to keep her distance. She didn't want Libby getting sick, as well.

"I'm using your computer. Don't worry," she assured him quickly, anticipating his protest. "I won't destroy anything. I'll even uninstall my program when I'm finished. But since I can't be two places at once and I have to finish this presentation, I decided to commandeer your computer."

He didn't care about the computer. Right now, he felt too weak to make use of it anyway. And it was an easy matter to replace it if something fatal actually did occur.

"I wasn't going to say anything, except for thanks." His expression was rueful. "Doesn't seem nearly good enough."

She smiled at him just before she shut the door. "It's a start."

Evan didn't remember falling asleep. But the next time he woke up, the rain had stopped. And something else had started.

The rhythmic, soothing sound had been replaced by Libby's voice coming from right outside his door. She was begging Claire for a chance to come in. Evan was surprised at how firm Claire sounded, turning her down. It gave him the feeling that Claire really couldn't be budged once she made up her mind about something.

He couldn't help but admire that, even though he had a feeling it could be at his expense.

"Honey, I really need you to look after Rachel for me, and Mr. Quartermain is still sick. He has germs I don't want you getting."

"But you're getting them," he heard Libby protest. He could almost see her pout. In about twelve years, she would make one hell of a heartbreaker. And in another ten on top of that, she'd be a lawyer to be reckoned with, he judged.

"Mama's strong."

He'd vouch for that, he thought. And soft. Very soft. His mind began to drift as he allowed himself to imagine just how soft she could be.

"You could still get sick," Libby persisted.

Definitely lawyer material, Evan decided. He'd enjoy seeing Libby arguing a case.

"Then you can take care of me," Claire told her.

He could hear unadulterated joy in Libby's voice. "I can? Really?" She was probably hoping Claire would get sick, just a little, so she could get her mother to make good on her promise, Evan thought.

"Really. Now get back to Rachel. Remember, she needs you."

All traces of desire to come visit the patient had left her voice. "Yes, Mama."

If he strained, he could hear the sound of her feet thundering on the rug as she flew to her charge. For a tiny thing, she had heavy feet.

"You're good at that," he told Claire as she walked into the room. "Reasoning with her instead of just telling her to obey."

He had absolutely no idea about parenting, but in his opinion, she had it down pat.

"Kids react to respect, the same as adults." Claire set down the tray she was carrying on his bureau. "Okay, it's time to get you back among the living. I have the classic healer for you." She gestured at the bowl in the center of the tray. "Chicken soup. Plus apple juice and some tea," she offered in a quick rundown, then flashed a mischievous smile. "And if you're very good, I'll let you have some gelatin for dessert. Cherry."

So saying, she placed the tray on his bed. Evan eyed the

soup. "I don't like chicken soup. They always make it too salty."

Now that he was getting better, he was being difficult. Why didn't that surprise her?

"Well, 'they' didn't make it," she informed him. "I did. And mine isn't too salty."

He didn't think anyone in his generation cooked anymore. His mother lamented that it was a lost art. His sisters knew how to boil water and how to dial for takeout.

"You made it?"

She lifted her chin, pretending to be affronted. "Don't look so surprised—I can cook."

Now that he thought of it, the soup did smell good. But how had she managed to make it? "I don't have anything in my refrigerator."

"The chicken's on loan from mine, okay?" She held out the spoon to him. "Now shut up and eat. You need to get your strength back."

And he knew just what he wanted to do with it when it returned.

Capitulating to the aroma and the vague hunger rumbling through his belly, he took the spoon from her. "All right."

"Attaboy, you'll be up and about in no time." Deciding that he couldn't sit up the way he was, she shifted the tray back to the bureau. "Of course, you can't eat like that unless I bring you a straw."

She remedied the problem by rearranging the pillows until they were all behind him. As he sat up, Evan's head began to swim unexpectedly, and he grabbed her arm to steady himself. It surprised and embarrassed him to discover just how weak he still was.

She stiffened slightly as his fingers accidentally brushed against the side of her breast. Claire felt her stomach tighten as taut as a high wire.

"Sorry," he apologized. "I didn't realize just how weak I was."

"You just need to eat something," she murmured self-consciously. She was acting like a schoolgirl. Struggling to hide her nerves, she set the tray in front of him again, then sat down on the other side. "I can make the plane go into the hangar if you're too weak to feed yourself."

It was tempting to have her feed him, not because he felt weak, but because he liked having her fussing over him. Liked it far more than he would have believed only a few days ago.

"No, I think I can handle my own hangar."

"Okay, Ace, call me if you need me." She began to rise.

"Why don't you stay and talk to me?" he asked. "Tell me about the project you're working on," he suggested when she looked as if she was going to beg off with an excuse.

Well, this was a surprise. Claire slowly sat down again. "All right. It's a logo for Aesthetic Athletics," she began. "There's this guru sitting in the middle, wearing a huge pair of running shoes. He's meditating about being in the Olympics...."

Chapter Nine

Libby stopped for breath, waiting. When her mother didn't say anything, Libby cocked her head and looked at her.

Mama had a funny look on her face, like she was a jillion miles away. Libby tugged on her sleeve to get her attention.

"Mama, Mama, aren't you listening to me?"

Fresh from putting Rachel to bed, a task that seemed to drain her of most of her energy, Claire had returned to the living room and sunk down on the sofa. Just in time. Her legs felt as if they'd given way.

Libby's voice was fading in and out of the buzzing in her ears.

"Hmm?" How could she be on a roller coaster when she was sitting still? Claire tried to concentrate on her daughter, but it wasn't easy. "I'm sorry, honey, I think I'm just going to lie down for a minute, all right?"

And then Claire stretched out, right where she sat, collapsing against the dark blue sofa like a balloon that had had all its air suddenly released.

Libby stood looking at her mother. Something was

wrong. Mama never lay down during the day. And she always listened to her, even when she looked as if she wasn't. Libby started to feel strange, funny, like there were all these big butterflies in her stomach trying to get out at once.

She shook her mother by the shoulder, wanting her to get up again. "Mama?"

Claire drew a long breath and let it out again, trying to regain ground. It didn't work. Ground was quickly slipping away from her.

It was just because she was pushing herself too hard— that's all. All she needed was a few minutes to rest and she'd be good as new.

"Just for a minute," Claire repeated. Her voice echoed in her head, sounding as if it were coming from deep inside a well. "I promise I'll be up and listening to you in a minute."

Shutting her eyes, Claire curled up on the sofa, bringing her knees to her chest almost reflexively. She felt cold and hot at the same time and didn't know if she wanted to get something to cover herself with or to change her sweater for something lighter. It was a moot point. Either choice involved moving, getting up. And she didn't have the strength to do that.

She would in a minute, she felt certain, but not right now. Right now, it was all she could do to concentrate on breathing.

"Mama?" Libby whispered. The butterflies got bigger.

Puzzled, worried, Libby turned on her heel and raced up the stairs to where she knew Rachel's daddy was. He wasn't as good as Mama, but he was a grown-up and grown-ups knew what to do.

She hadn't been allowed into his room the past four days because he was sick, but she knew it was okay to talk to him now. Mama said it was okay. Last night, Mama had let him come downstairs and eat with them at the table instead of taking a tray up to him the way she did before.

Mama had made a joke, and then he had made a joke right back and they had all laughed. Even Rachel, because when she laughed, she made bubbles. Libby liked that feeling, having a daddy at the table to laugh with. Mama didn't know, but she had pretended, just for a little bit last night, that Mr. Q. was her daddy, too, and Rachel was her sister.

Maybe if she pretended hard enough, they would be.

Mama had always told her to believe in dreams because dreams came true sometimes. And Mama was never wrong.

It was good to get dressed again, to feel something besides pajamas rubbing against his skin. The life of a layabout just wasn't for him. He felt restless when he wasn't doing something.

Although he had to admit that these past few days, after he'd gotten over being so weak, hadn't been all that bad. He'd had time to read and to think. A great deal of time to think and reflect on the life that was whizzing by him as he was working.

He'd missed a lot of it, he decided. He'd been so caught up in being the best, in doing his best, he hadn't had time to enjoy anything being the so-called best garnered him. If you took away the work, his life was pretty empty.

Or had been, he thought, up to a couple of weeks ago.

Evan tucked his shirt into his waistband and then stopped. He was being watched. He could feel it. Something Devin had said about a prickly feeling dancing along his neck whenever he was being watched came back to him. He was experiencing that same sensation now. Maybe they did have more in common than he thought.

Turning, Evan expected to see Claire leaning against the doorjamb, her eyes laughing at something he didn't fathom, a quirky little smile playing on her lips. the way it usually did.

Instead, he found a junior edition of her peering in.

It wasn't like Libby to just stand there, looking undecided. Libby always came racing into a room as if she were running across a field, intent on getting her kite airborne. But she was just standing there now. And there were signs of confusion on her small face instead of the usual unbridled joy he was quickly becoming accustomed to seeing.

Something was up, he thought. Evan sat down on his rumpled bed, his socks in his hand. He looked at her and smiled. "Hi."

Libby took his greeting to be an invitation to come in and she did, he noted, with somewhat less than her usual vigor.

It was funny what a few days flat on your back could do, he thought, pulling on one sock, then the other. He welcomed her company now where he had once cringed at it.

"Mama said you weren't catchy, so I can come in," Libby felt compelled to inform him. She was afraid he might send her away before she could tell him about Mama going to sleep in the middle of the day.

"That's right, I'm not 'catchy' anymore." He looked around for his shoes, then glanced at her. She had a very solemn expression on her face. It wasn't like her. That he had become a semiexpert on her behavior didn't even strike him as odd. "How are you doing?"

Libby answered the way her mother had taught her to reply to an inquiry of this nature. "Very well, thank you."

His shoes in sight, Evan remained on the bed. This didn't sound like Libby at all. Evan patted the place beside him for her. "Are you sure? You look a little puzzled."

Libby was quick to sit down next to him. She blew out a breath.

Just like her mother, he thought. This was probably what Claire had looked like as a little girl. He wondered if she'd had as much energy as Libby and then laughed silently at his own foolish question. Dynamos didn't sprout overnight.

"Mr. Q., why isn't Mama listening to me?"

He thought of telling her to call him Evan and decided to save that for another conversation. Right now, she had come to him with a problem. That, in itself, seemed like a milestone. That he wanted to help was another, if he were to stop to think of it.

"I don't know, Libby, maybe she just has a lot on her mind. You know, it hasn't been easy on her, taking care of all of us, you, me, Rachel, and doing her own work, as well."

He was accustomed to working long, grueling hours, but he didn't come home to a little girl to take care of or a house to clean. He had cleaning service for the latter. If he had to do it all himself, he didn't think he could manage. He didn't know how Claire did it and remained cheerful in the bargain. When did she get time to sleep?

"I help with Rachel," Libby interrupted. "I can diaper her good now, as long as Mama cleans her up first. It's icky." She made a horrible face, holding her stomach and sticking out her tongue in a grimace.

He laughed, which made her laugh in turn. The light sound made him think of tiny wind chimes shifting in the breeze.

"I know what you mean. Is your mother with Rachel?" He was actually surprised that Claire hadn't come in by now. She was always on Libby's heels.

Her hair flew to and fro as Libby adamantly shook her head. "No, Rachel's sleeping. Mama's in the living room. On the sofa."

"You mean she's actually sitting down?" Would wonders never cease?

Evan rose and retrieved his shoes, stepping into the loafers. He wanted to go downstairs and join Claire. If she was sitting down, so much the better.

Libby shook her head again. "No, she's kinda lying down."

Evan looked at Libby. "Lying down? Your mother?" An uneasiness began to nudge itself forward. "Are you sure?"

Libby's eyes narrowed as a frown took her face. "I know what lying down is," she protested, insulted. "And Mama's doing it. Right now."

Maybe Claire was just tired, he thought. But he had his doubts. "Let's go check her out, shall we?" He held out his hand to Libby.

Libby bounced off the bed, wrapping her fingers around his hand.

"What's the matter?" she asked as they went down the stairs.

Why was Mr. Q. all nervous? She could feel the butterflies getting stronger in her tummy again. She had come to him hoping he could make them go away, not make them bigger.

There was no need to alarm Libby. If she was frightened, she would just get in his way. Besides, this was probably all just nothing. Claire was undoubtedly just resting. Even the toughest batteries needed to be recharged once in a while.

"Nothing, I just thought of something I wanted to tell your mother."

The answer placated Libby. "That you're okay, huh? Mama took good care of you," she said with pride, puffing up her chest. "Mama takes good care of everybody."

"Not everybody," he contradicted. "I don't think Mama takes such good care of Mama." As a matter of fact, he knew it.

When he saw Claire slumped over on the sofa, the first thing Evan thought was that she had fainted. Dropping Libby's hand, he hurried over to Claire. Kneeling beside her, Evan raised Claire's head. She was paler than he'd ever remembered seeing her. Perspiration plastered her hair to her forehead and cheeks.

Evan brushed it away from her face, struggling with concern. He wasn't equipped to handle flesh-and-blood emergencies, only the paper kind.

Claire's eyes fluttered open, and she bit back a groan. "Just taking a nap," she mumbled.

"Nap, my as—asphalt," he amended, glancing at Libby. The little girl was staring at both of them with huge eyes. "Claire, you're sick."

"I am not," she protested weakly. "I'm fine. I'm just a little tired—that's all. Just let me lie here and close my eyes for a minute."

Her face was flushed and shining with perspiration. She was miles past "a little tired." Gently shaking her shoulder, he forced Claire to look at him. Evan raised four fingers. "How many fingers am I holding up?"

She squinted, trying to make them out through watery eyes.

"Three," she answered. "And I wish you'd stop wiggling them at me."

He dropped his hand, frowning. This time, her stubbornness wasn't going to help her. If nothing else, he was stronger than she was. "That does it, you're going to bed."

Making a last-ditch attempt at dignity and strength, Claire grabbed on to the arm of the sofa, using it for leverage. She meant to vehemently protest his declaration.

Or tried to. But even her resolve dissolved in the heat of the fever that was spinning its web through her body.

"I am not." She drew herself up to her feet.

Her words would have carried more weight if her legs

could have. But they buckled, both of them, and she pitched face forward into his arms, struggling against the darkness that threatened to consume her.

"Mama!" Libby screamed, alarmed.

"She's all right," Evan reassured the little girl in as calm a voice as he could muster. "She just needs some rest." Still holding her, he drew her closer to him. "Don't you, Claire?"

"Rest," she repeated as if it were the beginning of a healing mantra. And then she remembered what she had done when he had passed out. She gritted her teeth, fighting to stay conscious. "Just don't...get any ideas...about dressing me for bed."

He couldn't resist. "Turnabout is fair play." The alarm that momentarily flared in her eyes made him relent. This wasn't the time to tease her, although he was surprised that he actually had that inclination. The last time he'd felt like teasing a girl, he had been in third grade.

"You're obviously a lot more lucid than I was in your place. I'll take out a pair of pajamas, and you can put them on yourself." And then he smiled at her. "Spoilsport."

"Eat your heart out," she mumbled weakly.

"I am."

With that, Evan scooped her up into his arms. She felt, he thought, lighter than his briefcase usually did.

"No." Her protest sounded incredibly feeble, even to her. "You can't do that."

"I just did," he countered. Turning, Evan crossed to the stairs. He didn't have to look over his shoulder to know that Libby was right behind him like a faithful shadow. "She's going to be fine, Libby." He hoped his voice carried enough conviction to soothe the little girl's fears.

"You can't do this," Claire repeated. "You're sick, weak."

"No, I'm not." Evan tried not to think how good she

felt against him like this. "You're a great nurse. I feel fine, really. Except, maybe a little guilty that I've repaid your kindness by infecting you."

"Wasn't your fault," she murmured against his throat, her breath sending ripples through him.

Evan's stomach tightened into a hard ball. It wasn't right, having these kinds of feelings about a woman too sick to know what she was doing to him.

"Is Mama gonna be all right?"

He could hear the tightness in Libby's throat, as if there were tears forming. "She's going to be just fine, Libby," he assured her again.

"Yes, she is." Libby said the words loudly, as if to convince herself, as well. "And I'm gonna take care of her."

"We both will," Evan said before he even stopped to think about it. He realized that he meant it.

Very gently, he laid her down on his bed. His concern grew. She looked as pale as the case on his pillow.

Claire arched, her back aching. She should be getting up, she thought. Her body remained where it was, unwilling and unable to obey any command she might have given it.

But she could still protest. "You have work," Claire mumbled in his general direction. Her eyes shut again. The light was beginning to hurt.

He shrugged, keeping his voice light more for Libby's benefit than Claire's. "Like you said, I have a computer. And Donovan said not to come back until I was well. Maybe I'll have a relapse for a few days."

With luck, she would be better by then. At least, he could hope so.

Claire sighed, not really hearing him. "That's nice."

She barely had enough strength to climb into the pajamas that Evan had laid out for her and then drag herself into his bed. Logically, she knew she should have gone to her own. But her house and her bed seemed a million miles from here right now, and all she wanted to do was close her eyes and sleep.

Or die, whichever came first.

It was sleep.

And when she woke up again, there were a hundred little men in steel-pointed shoes line-dancing through her head. It was all Claire could do to pry open her eyes.

The room was dark. Was it raining again? Or was it night? She couldn't tell.

What she did know was that she didn't have time for this. She had things to do, a child to care for. A presentation to deliver. At least she'd had the presence of mind to print it all out when she'd finished it last night.

But it did her little good, sitting on Evan's desk downstairs while she was lying up here, in his bed.

She had to get up.

Shaking, she reached out to snap on the light. She missed the lamp and knocked over something that was in her way. Whatever it was hit the floor with a thud that registered with the hundred little men and sent them into another round of frenzied dancing across her skull and forehead.

Claire groaned and held her head as she sat up. She knew if she didn't hold it, it would fall off and roll away.

Light came in from the hallway, assaulting her, slicing through the wounds in her head that the pointy shoes had left in their wake.

"Get back into bed," Evan ordered.

Her hand wrapped around one post, she was still trying to get out. She had more of a chance of turning into a frog.

"But this is your bed." He belonged in it, not her. What if he wanted to share it? She must be really sick, she realized, because the thought of him lying beside her didn't make her nervous. It would have made her smile if she felt able to. Which she didn't.

Was she afraid he was going to take advantage of the situation? Not that he hadn't thought of it, but he'd quickly dismissed it. Then he'd thought of it again with a longing that no longer surprised him.

But there was no way he was going to do anything she didn't want.

"Don't worry." He pried her hand off the bedpost with the greatest of ease and placed it back on top of the covers, the way Libby might have arranged one of her dolls' limbs. "I'm staying in one of the guest rooms until you get well."

This wasn't right. She should be sitting up, not lying back. Why wasn't her body obeying?

"I wasn't worried about that. I was..." She felt exhausted. "I've got things to do." She exhaled the words breathlessly.

Yeah, right, he thought. It looked as if Claire Walker had finally met her match. And it was something so tiny, it wasn't even visible to the naked eye.

A little like love, he caught himself thinking.

"Like what?" he asked brusquely, attempting to clear his mind.

He sounded angry with her, she thought. Why shouldn't he be? He didn't want to take care of Rachel, and here he was, stuck with a sick woman in his bed and two children outside it.

"I've got to—got to take care of Libby. And Rachel."

Even sick, she thought of them first, he marveled. Whoever Rachel's mother was had tossed her away like a used tissue, and Claire was worrying about caring for a child who wasn't hers. The word *remarkable* occurred to him.

"Done and done," he said matter-of-factly. "They're fed, one of them is changed and both of them are happy. Next?"

She flicked her tongue over her lips, but they remained stubbornly dry. "My work..."

Now, that really surprised him. "You were the one who preached to me that work wasn't going to run away if I missed it for a few days."

"Yours won't," she corrected. She tried to prop herself up on her elbows again, but this time he pulled them out from under her, forcing her down. As if she needed help to fall flat. "Mine's on Rollerblades," she insisted. "If I don't get that presentation in, someone else'll get the job."

She caught his attention. He understood things like that. "When's your deadline?"

"Tomorrow." She said it as if it were a death sentence. She didn't have a prayer of being well by then. He thought a moment. When she had told him about the project, she'd mentioned the corporate home office was located in San Francisco. It was an easy matter to look the address up.

"Is it finished?"

She knew what he was getting at. Or thought she knew. Right now, she wasn't really sure of anything.

"Yes. I printed it out but I can't mail it in. It has to be brought in in person." And she was the person to bring it. Except that she was as weak as a flea.

"I wasn't going to suggest mailing it." He knew he could hire a courier to deliver it, but presentations such as Claire's needed the personal touch. "I'll take it in for you. It's the least I can do." He owed her that. And more.

Claire blinked. The fever was affecting her hearing. "You?"

He laughed at the incredulous expression on her face. "Me. I feel like myself again, thanks to you." Actually, that wasn't true. He felt better than himself, thanks to her.

It would have been an answer to a prayer, but there were complications. Two of them.

"The girls—" She wasn't all that sure she could take care of them, and he couldn't very well take them with him. He'd never make it there. He wouldn't last five minutes with both of them once he was outside the house.

Evan shrugged, the height of nonchalance. "I'll take them with me."

Now she knew she was hearing things. He couldn't have possibly said what she thought he said. The Evan Quartermain she knew would have sooner stuck his head into a lion's mouth than ventured outside with two children under the age of five.

"You?"

He vaguely wondered if he should be taking affront to her lack of faith, then chalked it up to the state her mind was in right now.

"I can handle it," he assured her. If his own words rang a little hollow, well, that was for him to worry about, not her. The only thing she had to worry about was getting well.

Claire would have argued with him if she had the strength, but just talking had evaporated what little she had managed to collect.

"All right, thank you." She tried to moisten her lips again with the same lack of success. Claire looked at him uncertainly. "You're sure?"

"I'm sure." I *hope*. "Now," he continued with more authority, "in the words of a very bossy woman I know, get some rest."

He didn't have to tell her twice. Mercifully, she slipped away from the center of the fire before he had a chance to say anything further.

Evan shook his head as he placed the comforter over Claire's shoulders. Then he squared his own and hoped that he was equal to the task he'd just set up for himself.

He did the only logical thing—he got help. He enlisted Libby in his cause.

Libby loved being treated like a big girl, and there was

nothing she loved better than being told what a help she was. It made her strive to live up to the praise. Evan had picked that much up by listening to Claire talk to the girl. He figured that between the two of them, they could handle Rachel and he could handle venturing out into the world with both of them, even if he felt himself outnumbered.

Claire's body ached when she woke up the next morning. She thought of calling for Evan, then tried to summon the strength to get up to look for him. It still just wasn't there.

Today, Claire knew, was not going to be a good day.

The day got worse when she saw the note on the comforter.

Evan had left her a note. Was he gone? Had Libby and Rachel proved to be too much for him to handle sanely? A queasiness overtook her as she blinked, clearing her eyes, and read.

Took your presentation to Aesthetic Athletics. The kids are with me. Be back soon.

Evan

The queasiness grew to full-fledged proportions. Claire had absolutely no idea when "soon" was. Only that it couldn't possibly be soon enough.

Chapter Ten

It wasn't very often that Claire allowed optimism to slip through her fingers. At times, it was only her tenacious hold on the sentiment that saw her through. Like when Jack had abandoned her.

She went through her pregnancy without the support of a husband or lover, or even a family. If it wasn't for Dr. Richmond and the kindness of some of her father's friends, enormous hospital costs would have been added to the burdens that she already had. Libby was born premature and needed extra care. As she did for the first few days after the delivery. Dr. Richmond convinced her father's hospital to underwrite the costs and called it a gift.

She accepted gratefully. Claire overcame every obstacle thrown her way, taking them in stride and keeping her chin up, convinced that things would be better eventually.

With her baby at the college day care, which she paid for with her own volunteer services, Claire went on to get her degree, using up the last of the money her father had left her in the process.

There hadn't been much to begin with, despite his lofty standing in the medical community. Besides having a lousy bedside manner, her father also had a lousy sense of business. He invested in the wrong companies, and trusted the wrong people. What should have been a thriving estate for him to will to his daughter just barely managed to see her through school.

The sale of her parents' house provided for the down payment on her own. It didn't, however, provide for the subsequent monthly payments. What remained of the proceeds from their house was eaten up by unexpected outstanding debts that came to light, as well as by a letter demanding payment for back taxes that had been overlooked. Claire settled everything and was left with nothing.

Nothing but Libby, her house and her determination. It was enough.

But being sick had temporarily depleted her supply of hope and with it, her optimism. Claire could feel the Aesthetics account slipping through her fingers. There was no way she could land it now. The company wasn't going to smile upon a neighbor coming by with two children in tow to drop off her presentation on the receptionist's desk.

If Evan even made it.

Which led her to her more major concern. Where was he? Where were the children? She knew if Libby was back, she'd hear the sound of running feet echoing somewhere in the house. Libby could never be accused of being a quiet child, even when she slept.

Where was she?

Claire slid down farther in the bed, pulling the covers over herself, wishing she could at least fall into the mind-numbing abyss of unconsciousness.

She must have fallen asleep eventually, because the very next thing she knew, Libby was in the room, bouncing on the bed. Even in her present state, Claire welcomed the jarring motion. It took all the restraint she had not to hug her daughter.

"You did it, Mama, you did it." Libby leaned forward, peering into Claire's face. "Do you feel better now?"

"Did what, honey?" It disturbed her greatly that she could barely pick up her head. Instead of better, she was feeling worse.

And then Evan was in the room, taking Libby's hand. Taking Libby. "C'mon, Libby, you know you're not supposed to be in here."

His voice was gentle, kind. Or maybe that was just her delirium growing.

Libby was on the verge of tears. She didn't want to be separated from her mother again. "But she's my mama."

Evan sighed. The last thing he wanted was a scene, or to have Libby crying. But she couldn't stay here, either. Claire was still ill and besides needing her rest, she could still infect Libby.

He picked Libby up, holding her against him. She squirmed, then gave up.

"And she's going to continue to be your mama, but right now, she needs her rest, okay?" He could feel the indecision warring within the young body. Evan threw in what he hoped was his ace. It had worked before. "And I need your help with Rachel."

In the dim light, Claire could just about see Libby pouting over his shoulder as Evan carried her daughter out.

"Okay, I guess. But you tell me as soon as Mama's rested and better. Deal?"

"Deal," he promised.

"What did she mean?" Claire asked suddenly, hoarsely calling after Evan as Libby's words registered. "That I did it?"

Evan stopped in the doorway. Nothing pleased him more

than telling her this. "You got the account. Congratulations."

"That's nice," Claire murmured, and then slipped away again.

She thought she heard someone laugh, but couldn't be sure.

She dreamed it, knew she dreamed it. After all, it was a dream for her, to get the Aesthetic Athletics account. That had been lost to her because she had gotten sick tending to Evan.

Everything happened for a reason. She just didn't understand this one yet.

Didn't understand, either, why she and Evan were celebrating. Dancing somewhere high above, surrounded by clouds, with sunshine streaming through, bathing them both.

Sunshine had to be the reason she felt so warm in his arms. So aglow.

And then they weren't dancing anymore. They were kissing, holding each other tightly as if that were all that counted in the world. His kisses grew more ardent, more passionate.

She could feel the floodgates quaking, threatening to break within her. Threatening to flood her, not with water, but with emotions. Emotions she had struggled so hard to lock away after Jack had deserted her.

Emotions only hurt you.

But they didn't hurt now. They felt good. Wonderful.

Evan felt wonderful.

And her body felt like a rare violin, being played after having been kept in a dark case for so many years. It hummed.

There were angels watching them. No, not angels, Rachel and Libby, standing beside a mirror image of the two of them. Except that the mirror image was different somehow. It was her, but it wasn't her; him, but not him.

And they were smiling. Smiling at the pair kissing in the center of a dance floor made up of clouds. Smiling at her and Evan.

Suddenly, the girls vanished. Heat crept up her neck as she felt and watched the kiss blossom into something so powerfully potent, it made her head spin and her desire soar. He was undressing her, loving her with his hands, with his eyes, with his lips.

Loving her...

Claire woke up with a start, then dragged air into lungs that felt as if they had been completely depleted of oxygen.

Her pulse was beating wildly.

Momentarily disoriented, Claire looked around, expecting to see clouds. Expecting to see Evan. There were no clouds, no mirror images, no angels. No Evan. She wasn't even in her own bed. This wasn't her bedroom; it was Evan's.

Evan's.

Completely conscious now, Claire looked down at herself, fervently hoping that what she'd dreamed hadn't been reality. That they hadn't danced, hadn't kissed.

Hadn't...made love, she realized.

But she wasn't nude; she was wearing pajamas.

She didn't own pajamas....

It took her another moment to remember that they were his and that she had put them on just before she'd collapsed in his bed.

Claire sank back against her pillow. The red-hot, tingling sensation that had danced through her body was only now beginning to settle down. She could feel herself blushing.

They'd made love in her dream, she and Evan. That was why she felt as if her entire body was on fire. It wasn't the fever that was to blame; it was the dream. Claire touched her forehead. It was damp and warm, but not hot.

She wasn't delirious, just sick.

And turned on.

Claire drew in a few more breaths, forcing herself to calm down. She'd almost succeeded, and then negated it all by remembering the children.

Dear heaven, she'd been lying here in bed, having sensual dreams while the children were out there, with him. Who knew what they'd gone through? They were probably hungry and dirty and...

She had to get up and get to them. They needed her. Evan needed her.

Summoning her strength, Claire stumbled out of bed and made her way into the hall as best she could. The process was much too slow to satisfy her. Claire had to stop and hold on to the walls and then the doorjamb to steady herself.

Each time, the room rippled like a mirage in the blazing desert sun.

She finally made it into the hallway and inched her way along the walls. When she stopped concentrating on getting her balance, she realized that she was listening to Evan's voice.

He was reading something out loud. A story.

Bracing herself as she moved, Claire drew closer to the sound of his voice. The door was open, and she peered into the room.

He was sitting on a chair with Libby on his lap. The bed was turned down and waiting for her. Evan was patiently reading a story to Libby out of her favorite book.

He must have gone and gotten it from her room, Claire realized.

"...and the Prince and Cinderella lived happily ever after.'' Evan closed the book and then looked at Libby expectantly.

Libby wriggled in his lap. ''More, please,'' she begged.

This was beginning to be a familiar pattern, but he was up to it.

''No, you've got to make good on your promise. You said one more story and then you'd go to bed. I read the story, now you have to go to bed.'' He set her down on the floor.

The sigh was bigger than Libby. She pouted, but saw no way out. ''Okay, I guess.''

Evan pulled back the covers for her, waiting for her to get in. ''You bet okay. You want to grow up to be big and strong and pretty just like your mother, don't you?''

Libby scrambled into the bed. ''Mama's beautiful, not pretty,'' she corrected loyally.

Evan tucked the blanket around her and smiled, thinking of Claire. ''Yes, she is.''

Libby studied him with the same intensity that scientists examine microbes under a microscope. ''You like my mama?''

He'd discovered in the past few days that not much got by Libby. Since they were alone, he saw no reason to deny it. ''Yes, she's a very nice lady.''

She thought he liked her more than just nice. ''She's like Cinderella, isn't she?''

Evan pretended to look surprised. ''You mean she sews clothes for mice?''

He got the reaction he was after. Libby covered her mouth and giggled. ''No, silly. I mean she works real hard. *All* the time.'' She exaggerated the word on purpose.

He could see where Libby could draw the comparison. ''Yes, she certainly does.''

Encouraged by his agreement, Libby continued spinning her childlike web. ''She needs a prince to marry her.''

Evan could just hear what Claire would have to say about that comment. Claire had made it very clear that she was doing fine on her own. No princes for her. Which was a damn shame. Not that he was the prince type, but he wouldn't mind trying to take care of her once in a while. He discovered that he rather liked the feeling of caring for someone.

"I don't think your mother needs anything. She's a very independent lady."

It was what, Claire thought, she had striven for. What she would have wanted to hear someone say of her. So why did hearing it from Evan's lips make her feel so empty?

Libby still liked the idea of a prince. And so did Mama—she was sure of it. "Mama says everybody needs somebody, no matter who they are."

He paused, looking down at the little girl. He wondered if there was a hidden message in all this, or if he was just hoping there was. "Your mama is a very wise lady."

He was about to leave. Libby stopped him dead with her next question. "Will you be her prince?"

Evan laughed. Now, there was a role he wasn't qualified for. "I'm not anybody's idea of a prince."

Libby sat up. "You are mine," she told him enthusiastically. Momentum grew in her voice. "And Rachel's."

It was a simple fantasy and simple words, coming from a four-year-old. He had no idea why they should touch him so much. But they did.

"Rachel's too young to think or have an opinion," he told her softly. He tried to make her lie back, but she was like a spring that refused to stay in position.

"No, she's not. She thinks just like I do." Rachel was going to grow up just like her, Libby thought confidently. She just knew it.

Evan knew better than to argue with Libby. Diplomacy

was what was called for here. "Well, she's asleep right now, and so should you be."

Libby wanted to rub her eyes, but she clenched her hands into small fists on either side of her. Rubbing her eyes would make him think she was tired.

"I'm not sleepy. Really I'm not," she insisted. And then she raised hopeful eyes to his face. "Will you stay here till I fall asleep?"

He was tired, and there were things he still had to do. He'd hooked up with his office and should have been working on something for the past hour instead of sitting here and reading to Libby.

Evan nodded at the light switch. "How about if I leave the light on again?"

She didn't want the light. Lights didn't make monsters go away. Only grown-ups did. "No, stay. Please?"

There was an urgency in her voice he couldn't force himself to ignore. For some reason, she didn't want to be alone. It had been a long time ago, but he could vaguely remember being afraid of the dark.

"All right. But you have to promise you'll try very hard to fall asleep quickly."

She nodded her head vigorously. "I promise." She eyed the storybook on the chair. "I fall asleep faster if Mama reads to me."

He should have seen this one coming a mile away.

"Con artist." He laughed, shaking his head. "Libby, I think you're going to go all the way and become president someday."

She took the comment in stride, as her due. Presidents were important people who were in history books and got to talk on TV. It might be a nice job to have. She looked at him. "If I do, will you come and read to me, Mr. Q.?"

"Only if you don't call me Mr. Q. It makes me feel like a character on 'Star Trek.'"

"What's that?"

He couldn't believe she didn't know. "And here I thought your mother taught you everything. Libby, you're in for a treat. Tomorrow night, we're watching TV together."

"All right!" Scrambling forward, she hugged him, then scooted back under her covers. "What do you want me to call you?"

"How about 'Evan'?"

"Evan," she repeated with approval. "Will you come and read to me when I'm president, Evan?" she asked him again.

"You bet." Making himself comfortable on the bed, he picked up the book and began to read out loud.

Claire slipped slowly back into Evan's bedroom, a bemused smile on her lips.

And she had been worried....

He had begun to think that Libby was never going to fall asleep. It had taken another story and a half before Libby's eyes finally closed. His jaw felt tight from reading.

The wealth of patience he'd found within himself surprised Evan. As did the discovery of other feelings that were steadily coming to the forefront. Feelings he would have said only a short while ago that he didn't have, that he wasn't capable of. And most definitely, that he didn't need.

Feelings of love and attachment.

Oh, he cared about his own family. There wasn't anything he wouldn't do for his mother and for his sisters, Paige and Krystle. And yes, even for Devin. It wasn't so much that he'd actually disliked Devin when they were growing up as that he felt he was living in his brother's shadow. Outgoing, gregarious, Devin always managed to charm everyone he met. Everyone loved Devin. When they met Evan, who was more introverted and shy, they were surprised at the difference. And sometimes vocal about it.

Evan told himself he didn't need those kinds of things, that he could do without the friendships and the admiration, and that what mattered in life was success. He'd said it so often and so forcefully, he'd almost managed to fool himself.

Until now.

Until he'd been forced to take care of a chatterbox, a baby and a woman who was getting under his skin so far and so deep, there was a danger that he'd have to have her surgically removed before he could go on with his life.

What was his life, anyway? he wondered ruefully as he walked down the hall. Deadlines, presentations, facts, figures, a computer screen, people in meetings whose faces he didn't remember and a six-figure income.

Somehow, that didn't seem to add up to very much when measured in terms of what Claire had. Love. She and Libby were a unit. A unit that was calling to him, showing him what he was missing.

He wanted that unit in his own life. As part of his own life.

Evan stopped before the room where Rachel lay, hopefully sleeping. He debated checking on her, knowing that there was a fifty-fifty chance he would wake her if he opened the door. It was safer just to walk on and assume the best.

He decided to risk it.

Cracking the door slightly, he slowly pushed it open a fraction of an inch at a time. The odds, for once, were with him and the right fifty was in his corner. Rachel remained sleeping.

He crept softly into the room and then stood looking down at her. The room was quiet. If he listened, he could hear her breathing.

There was a dim light draping the room, coming from a children's lamp Libby had helped him find in Claire's garage. Evan was amazed at how helpful Libby actually was. A wry grin curved his mouth. She probably sensed how helpless he was without her.

He wondered if Claire could sense the same thing.

That was off limits, he told himself. Claire was off limits. She'd been helpful to him; he couldn't repay her by dragging her further into his life. What woman would want to get mixed up with a man with a baby on a permanent basis, especially since she already had a child of her own?

A child of her own. Was Rachel his own? He didn't know; he truly didn't know. He did know that he hadn't wanted her to be. In the beginning. But now it was different. Now he woke up in the middle of the night to her cry. Her silence woke him just as much as her cries did. He was tuned into her internal clock, had made it his.

When he'd asked Devin to find Rachel's mother, it was in hopes that he could get her to confess that Rachel wasn't his and to take her back. Now he wanted to find her so that he could get legal custody.

It was a startling thing to realize that a man as large as he could be held so fast by a hand as tiny as hers. Held by her hand, and by Libby's and Claire's. They had all taken a piece of him without his knowing it. A piece he knew he didn't want back.

Not that he had anything to offer Claire that she needed. If there was ever a woman who was all together, it was her.

"But maybe you and I can have something, hmm?" he whispered to Rachel.

To his surprise, she opened her eyes for a moment. And then a dreamy little look passed over her face, and her eyes slid shut again.

His heart twisted in his chest. Hearts always twisted

when they were being removed. He didn't have to open Rachel's hand to know that was where his heart now resided.

Very quietly, he slipped out and closed the door behind him.

Chapter Eleven

"And just where do you think you're going?"

Startled, Claire turned around in the hallway to see Evan standing behind her. She'd been so preoccupied when she left the bedroom, she hadn't heard him walking toward her.

"Downstairs. I've got to get the turkey out of my freezer and find a way to defrost it quickly." There wasn't much hope there. She knew the bird was rock solid. Maybe there was still one available at the supermarket. Time had strung itself out into one long chain, and she'd lost track of the days, but that was still no excuse to forget what today was.

Claire flushed. "I forgot that today is Thanksgiving," she admitted.

It was nice to see color back in her cheeks that wasn't associated with a fever. It was even nicer to be able to ride to her rescue.

"The turkey's already defrosted and about one-third on its way to being baked. *Some* of us didn't forget," he told her loftily.

As he had returned home from Aesthetic Athletics headquarters, Evan had made up his mind to cook the meal. Feeling triumphant at securing the account for her, he'd made a quick stop at the grocery store, or as quick as it could be with two children in tow, and picked up everything he remembered seeing on his mother's table during past Thanksgivings.

Claire stared at him as if he'd just announced he was Peter Pan and about to undertake a journey to Neverland. "You're making Thanksgiving dinner?"

"*We* are," he corrected. "Libby's helping." The little girl insisted on being part of everything he did. He was getting very accustomed to that. "Actually, she does a lot of ordering around." He raised an eyebrow, looking at Claire pointedly. "Can't figure out where she could have gotten that from."

Claire hadn't progressed beyond his earlier statement. Try as she might, she couldn't picture him in the kitchen doing anything other than preparing coffee. "You're making Thanksgiving dinner?"

He smoothed out the furrow between her eyebrows with the tip of his finger. "I thought we just got past that. That fever must have sucked out more of your brain cells than I anticipated."

Why was he doing this? It went far above and beyond repaying a debt he thought he owed. Caring for her, putting up with Libby, *reading* to Libby—it was all miles beyond the call of any duty she was certain Evan was acquainted with.

"Don't you have a family to go to? Mother? Sisters? Your twin brother?" He'd mentioned that they all lived in southern California. Evan should have been on his way there with Rachel last night, not here with her.

And yet here he was.

Something warm and hopeful began to bloom within her. This was going to be the first holiday meal he'd miss

sharing with his family, but he'd made his choice and figured he knew where he belonged. "They all have each
other. I thought someone should stay and take care of the
girls and you."

The girls and you. It had such a lovely sound to it, Claire
mused. With very little effort, she could get really involved
with this man. Who was she kidding? She was already involved with this man.

But he didn't have to know that.

She bit her lip. It was only fair she make the offer, even
if she hoped he wouldn't take her up on it. "You don't
have to. I mean, I feel better now and I could look after
Rachel if you wanted to get away."

He didn't remember taking her into his arms, only remembered wanting to. But here she was, against him. As
she should be.

"Maybe I don't want to get away." He brushed the hair
away from her face.

Her bangs always seemed to be falling into her eyes, he
thought. It gave her an elfin quality that belied the strength
that was beneath and allowed him to pretend that she
needed someone. Needed him.

"Maybe I'm just where I want to be. Here, getting my
fingers burned, making really bad mashed potatoes and
looking into the eyes of the most incredible woman I've
ever met."

He wasn't going anywhere. She felt her heart surge.
"Maybe the fever burned out more of *your* brain cells than
anticipated."

Evan shook his head. There was nothing wrong with his
thinking process. Finally, there was something very right
about it.

"No, it just burned away the plastic casing that blocked
anything good from coming in."

Leaning into him, Claire lifted her chin, an invitation in

her eyes. "I'm not catchy anymore." Then she realized that he probably didn't know what she was saying. "That's Libby-talk for—"

"I know what it means." He feathered his hand along her cheek. Her skin felt like cream. And she felt like heaven against him. "She used the line on me. Does that mean I can kiss you?"

The heart that had been hammering so wildly just a second before stopped altogether. "That's what it means. Are you going to?"

The smile was slow as it moved along his lips, and so wildly sensual, Claire couldn't breathe. "I'm thinking about it."

If Evan didn't kiss her soon, she was going to have to force herself on him. "Don't make me get nasty with you."

The smile became a grin and all the more sexy for it. "I love it when you get physical."

And then Evan brought his lips down to hers and kissed her the way he couldn't for the past few days. The way he'd ached to.

The wait had made the reward all the more sweet. As soon as he kissed her, he could feel his blood surging through his body, hot and demanding. This was the woman he wanted in his life. The woman who was going to matter. Who already did matter.

Desire coiled like a spring that had been set, eager for release. The degree of intensity surprised him. Physical attraction had always been a pleasurable thing, but it had always been something he could walk away from if he chose. Now there was no choice. He couldn't have crawled away on his knees if he wanted to.

He wanted to be with her, to love her the way he knew she needed to be loved. The way he needed to make love with her.

Clamping down restraints before they completely disintegrated, he drew back from her. "Nothing wrong with your lips, that's for sure."

"Is Mama all better?"

The high-pitched, inquisitive voice parted them more effectively than his resolve did. Evan smiled as he looked toward her. Libby was standing at the landing, eyeing them both and looking as pleased as he felt.

"All better, Libby," Claire murmured, wondering how long it would take for her pulse to settle down to normal.

It was all Libby needed to hear. She hurried over to her mother, linking her small fingers through Claire's and tugging her toward the stairs. "Then you can come and help." Libby stood up on her toes and whispered, "Evan's making the potatoes all lumpy."

Claire didn't want close proximity to annul the good manners she'd worked hard to instill in Libby. "Honey, his name is Mr. Quartermain."

"He told me I could call him Evan because if I don't, he'll be a man from outer space." She looked up at Evan for confirmation, but he was laughing too hard to provide it.

Claire was left to wonder just what had gone on while she had been sick. "I'm sure there's a translation to this," she told Evan. At least she hoped so. "Why don't you explain it all to me while I'm unlumping your potatoes?"

He put his hand on hers as she began to go down the stairs. "Are you sure you're up to this?"

Claire stopped and smiled at him. His concern was touching and almost worth getting sick as a dog for. "I told you, I'm fine." Her tongue moved along the outline of her lips, tasting him again. She felt the shiver of a thrill dance down her spine. "And ridiculously giddy, considering I'm out of work."

Evan stared at her. Had he missed something? "How do you figure that?"

She really didn't want to talk about it now, even though she'd been the one to bring it up. Today was too perfect to spoil.

Turning, she walked down the stairs with Libby leading the way. She didn't want him to read the disappointment in her eyes.

"Well, I lost the Aesthetics account, and I don't have anything else on tap right now." She shrugged. "But something'll come up." Claire maintained a cheerful voice for Libby's sake. And her own. "It always does."

He still didn't understand. "How did you manage to lose the Aesthetics account? They just gave it to you two days ago."

It was her turn to stare at him. It took concentration to keep her mouth from falling open. "They just...? When?"

There was a definite glitch in communication here, Evan thought. Maybe she didn't know. He'd been surprised she hadn't said anything to him about it, but thought it was because she was low-key when it came to success. Unlike him.

"The day I went to make your presentation. I told you when I came back that you had it."

She had it. She had the account. Her eyes grew huge. He wasn't kidding. Claire was stunned and too happy and relieved for words. "Then it's true? I wasn't just dreaming?"

He laughed, shaking his head. That was why she hadn't said anything. She didn't know. "No. They were very impressed with your work."

Evan didn't bother telling her that he had gone to school with the head of the Aesthetic Athletics marketing department and had wangled a one-on-one meeting to make sure that Claire's work got the priority consideration it deserved. Telling her would only take away some of her thunder, and she deserved all of it.

Besides, he was being sufficiently compensated. He loved watching the way her eyes lit up.

"I've got a check for you they drew up on the spot to make sure that you wouldn't take this logo to another company. Formal contracts will be in the mail the first of the week," he informed her. "You're to consider yourself part of their staff from here on in—for as long as you want," he added, knowing how much freedom meant to her.

When Evan's words finally sank in, Claire let out a whoop of joy and impulsively threw her arms around him. "Really?"

His arms encircled her automatically. "Really." He liked holding her like this, feeling her heart beat against his. Funny how important the simple things in life could be, now that she was in it.

There was something he wanted to know, a question her words had raised. Still holding her, he cupped her cheek softly and asked, "When you said you thought it was just a dream—does that mean you dream about me?"

A smile teased her lips, slipping up to her eyes. "Maybe."

It was hard to imagine a thirty-year-old man's stomach tightening over something so tenuous as a *maybe*. But it did. "Often?"

Very smoothly, she disentangled herself from him, the same smile playing on her lips. "Don't sap my strength with interrogations, Mr. Quartermain—I have potatoes to rescue."

Claire walked into the kitchen and saw that Rachel was sitting in her high chair, happily making a mess of what had been breakfast. She was smearing squashed bananas and what looked to be strained peaches all along the formerly white tray.

"Looks like someone's getting creative," Claire noted. He picked up a towel and began wiping the sticky fingers, wondering if he was fast enough to keep Rachel from making them messy again before he could clean up the tray.

"My sister Paige loves to paint. Maybe she gets it from her." There was an odd expression on Claire's face as she looked at him. "What?"

Claire grabbed a paper towel and did the honors on the tray. She had no idea why her throat felt as if it was tightening. This was a happy moment, not a sad one. "That's the first time I've heard you actually refer to Rachel as being yours."

He didn't want to make a big deal out of it. Except that it was. *She* was. If not for Claire, Rachel would have been the single biggest deal of his life, Evan realized.

"Yeah, well, I've decided this is probably on the level." He tossed the streaked towel on the counter. "If it was some kind of a hoax, then Rachel's mother would be asking for money instead of abandoning her. Besides," he added, looking down at the round little face, "Rachel does look a lot like my sisters did when they were her age."

"You remember?" Claire pulled a second paper towel off the rack and moistened it. "You're a lot more sensitive than I gave you credit for."

He debated letting her think that, but he had always believed that honesty was the only cornerstone to use in laying a foundation, and this foundation was too important to jeopardize for the sake of ego points.

"Not to shatter my new image, but my mother likes to drag out family albums on any pretext at any time. I've seen pictures of my sisters when they were around Rachel's age countless times. She has their eyes. Green and beautiful."

"She has *your* eyes," Claire corrected.

He shrugged self-consciously as he gave Rachel the ring of keys she loved to play with. "Men don't have beautiful eyes."

She'd embarrassed him, Claire thought. Now, why was that so hopelessly endearing? "You do. It was my first hint that you were human after all."

She'd piqued his interest. He liked the way the conversation was going. "What was your second?"

Instead of answering, she cast a sidelong glance at her daughter, busy solemnly stirring what would eventually be a pie filling. Her meaning was clear. She couldn't talk in front of Libby.

This was becoming more encouraging by the minute. He could wait.

"Okay, on to other things," Evan announced. Producing a grocery bag he hadn't emptied out yet, he deposited the contents onto the only space on the table that didn't have a bowl or a box or some ingredient for the feast occupying it. Yams came tumbling out. Two broke in half on contact. Evan wondered if that was bad. "What do we do with these things to make them edible?"

Claire reached for another towel and tucked it around her waist like an apron. "Looks like I got well just in time."

"This had to be the nicest Thanksgiving I can remember in a long, long time."

Claire's words came out on a contented sigh. She was sitting curled up beside Evan on the sofa in the family room, watching flames dancing around a log in the fireplace.

The dinner had long since been consumed, the dishes washed and put away at her insistence. They had all fussed over Rachel, and then Evan had played with Libby while Claire put the baby to bed. By the time she'd come out again, she found that Evan had accomplished the impossible. He had actually exhausted Libby. She had crawled up beside them on the sofa, wanting to stay up "just a little longer.'' And had promptly fallen asleep five minutes after permission was granted.

The baby was sleeping; Libby lay with her head on Claire's lap. Claire's hand lingered protectively on Libby's shoulder, her own head leaning against Evan's. If this wasn't happiness, then she didn't know what was.

"Yeah, it was pretty nice, wasn't it?" Evan lazily stroked her arm. He couldn't remember ever feeling this sort of peace, and yet, it was held together with thin wires of excitement. Excitement generated by the same woman who filled him with this sense of peace.

It was far too complicated for him to try to unravel. Besides, he was unraveling pretty well himself right now. And finding a whole new person underneath.

Claire felt a little guilty that her happiness meant someone else's disappointment. "Think your family minds that you're here this year?"

Evan laughed to himself, hearing again what his mother had to say when he'd called to apologize. The offense ranked only a little below the start of World War II.

"My mother'll make me pay," he said, pausing to kiss her temple, "until she sees you."

Claire drew her head back to look at him. "Me? What do I have to do with it?"

How could she not know? "Everything." He'd intended on waiting for a more opportune moment, then decided that his whole life had been spent waiting and he didn't want to do that anymore.

"I want you to meet them. My family. I know they'll want to meet you and Libby." He grinned as he glanced at the sleeping child. She looked so deceptively calm this way. A dynamite stick in repose. "My mother has been after all four of us kids to get married and give her grandchildren. I thought I might give her a preview."

Not everyone was up to Libby's exuberance. "To make her eat her words?" Claire guessed.

Not if he knew his mother. After all, she'd raised the four of them, and they had never been a tranquil bunch. "She'll fall in love with Libby once she stops to catch her breath."

She raised her head again, almost afraid to guess at what he was saying. "Why should she fall in love with Libby?"

He traced her lips with his thumb, watching the way her eyes grew dark with desire. It was a sight, he knew, he was never going to tire of. "I thought that was obvious."

Something caught in her throat. Anticipation? Her heart? All she knew was that she couldn't swallow. "Sometimes," she said in a whisper, afraid her voice would break if she spoke any louder, "the most obvious things are missed and overlooked. Why don't you explain it to me?"

He wished he had Devin's gift. Devin was never at a loss as to what to say. "I'm not good with words, Claire, unless I'm putting them down in a report or a memo."

He wasn't going to get out of telling her that easily. "Okay, I can accept that. Write me a memo."

"What?"

"Write me a memo," she repeated. "Here, I'll start it for you." Claire pretended to write in the air. "'Claire!'" She looked at him. "Okay, you take it from there."

Amusement lifted the corners of his mouth. "What's the memo supposed to be about?"

She sighed. This might be more difficult than she anticipated. "Why you want to take us to meet your family. And why your mother is going to fall in love with Libby."

He settled back, draping his arm over her shoulder. "Well, my mother'll fall in love with Libby because you can't help falling in love with Libby."

"Did you?" she pressed.

It was his turn to tease her, and he rather enjoyed doing it. "Maybe."

"I'll take that as a yes," she decided. "Now, the first part." Turning, her face was a scant inch away from his. That would account for why her heart was beating so fast. "Why should we meet your family?"

Evan played out his line. "Because they're nice people."

"Okay," she allowed. "And why should they meet us? And if you say because we're nice people," she warned him, "I may be forced to hit you."

He could just picture that. "My, have you always had this violent streak?"

"Only with very stubborn men."

Evan nodded. "I'll have to remember that. They should meet you because, other than being very nice people," he said, grinning, "you've also become important to me."

It was like pulling teeth, but she wasn't about to stop now. "Important how? Important like a nanny or a housekeeper?"

He knew what she was after and he was enjoying himself. "A little more than that."

Claire raised her chin, her eyes narrowing. "How little?"

Evan flicked his finger down her nose. Damn, but she stirred him. And she had a right to know it. "All right, a lot more. Satisfied?"

"No," she sighed, "but we're getting there."

The smile on his lips grew serious. "Come up to my room and we'll see what we can do about the 'satisfied' part. We're both finally well enough to stay in the same bed at the same time." He couldn't begin to count how many times he'd thought about that in the past week.

Claire looked down at Libby, nestled so peacefully on her lap. "Evan..."

He could read her thoughts. "You're afraid she'll wake up and find us together?"

Maybe that sounded old-fashioned, but that was the way she wanted to raise Libby. With a good sense of values firmly entrenched. "Yes."

He pretended to consider that. "She might have to get used to it."

She didn't want to hurt him or spoil this. Any of it. But he had to understand her position—as difficult as it was for her to take. As much as she knew she loved him, she was still Libby's mother, and with that came a responsibility that had to take precedence over her heart.

"Evan, it's not that I don't want to. I do. For the first time in years, I really do, but Libby's too young to understand about the way it is between men and women." And it was up to her to protect Libby for as long as she could.

"Oh, I don't know about that." Lightly, he ran his hand over Libby's hair. It felt as silky as Claire's. "She's pretty savvy, and most kids understand that their parents sleep in the same bed."

"Parents?" Claire echoed dumbly. What did that have to do with what they were discussing?

She really didn't know, did she? He'd never met a woman as unassuming as Claire. "Yeah, you know, mother, father." He pointed to her, then jerked his thumb back to himself. "You, me."

Claire held up her hand. This was going way too fast for her to assimilate. "Hold it, hold it, what are you saying?"

Evan shrugged. "I told you I wasn't any good at talking." He gave it to her straight. "I'm asking you to marry me."

She knew how she felt about him, but she hadn't thought that he actually reciprocated these feelings. "When did this happen?"

"Just now. I just asked you if you'd marry me," he answered innocently.

She hit his shoulder with the flat of her hand. He was doing this on purpose.

"Not that, I mean when did you decide that you wanted to marry me?" If the signs had been there, she certainly hadn't seen them.

He didn't even ·have to think about it. "Somewhere in between my passing out on my bed and holding you in my arms in the hall this morning. Why, did I miss an entry deadline?"

She felt completely dazed. "No, it's just that…I didn't… That is…" Claire gave up. "You leave me completely speechless."

He sincerely doubted that, but for the sake of peace, he let it go. "That's good, because what I've got in mind doesn't need words. As a matter of fact, words only get in the way." He framed her face with his hands, becoming serious. "I love you, Claire. I don't need an answer right now—just tell me that you'll think about it."

There was that wild, heady feeling again. The one that took her breath away and made her pulse leap as if she were sprinting toward a finish line.

"Yes."

He searched her eyes, wanting an answer despite what he had just said. He knew he shouldn't push, but it was hard not to, not when he felt this way. "Then you'll think about it?"

"No."

Confused, he tried to decipher which question she had just answered. "You won't think about it?"

Obviously, he needed this spelled out. Claire began spelling. "The answer is yes, Evan. Yes, I will marry you."

He'd always been cautious and even now, he was afraid to take her reply and run with it. "This isn't just the fever talking, is it?"

"Yes." She laughed. "But it's not the kind of fever you

think. It's more of a slow roast, the kind I feel in my chest every time I see you. Every time I watch you with Rachel or hear you reading a story to Libby.''

The last surprised him. "When did you hear me reading to Libby?''

"When you read *Cinderella* to her.''

"That narrows it down,'' he quipped. "I've been reading *Cinderella* to her for the last four nights.'' He'd come to learn that it was one of the main staples of her nighttime routine.

Claire remembered every word she'd overheard perfectly. "The night you said I was beautiful.''

He'd thought he'd heard something in the hall that night, but he had chalked it up to his imagination. Now he knew it wasn't. "You eavesdropped?''

Claire preferred to think of it differently. "I thought I was coming to the rescue.'' She laughed at herself. "I was making my way down the hall, holding on to the walls. All in all, I'm glad you didn't see me.'' The smile lit up her face, already aglow in the firelight. "And I'm glad I heard you.''

"So am I.'' She was going to marry him. She'd said yes. He felt like celebrating, like announcing it from the rooftops, or better yet, e-mailing several million people with the news. "So what do you want to do? We have the whole night ahead of us.''

Claire sighed, snuggling against him. "Just sit here by the fire, listen to Libby breathe. Feel your heart against my cheek.''

"Funny, I was just going to suggest that.'' Evan's arm tightened about her shoulders as he brought his lips down to hers.

Chapter Twelve

"We get to do this two times this year, huh, Mama?" Libby beamed as she tossed another handful of tinsel at the Christmas tree.

"Yes, honey." Claire undid the last box of silvery streamers. She figured that four should do it, as long as Libby remembered to toss the tinsel on all sides. It wasn't a very big tree, but it was a Christmas tree, which was all that really counted.

"Why didn't Evan want to have one this year?" Another fistful sailed and landed in a clump around a ball depicting Santa and his reindeer.

From his complete lack of decorations, Claire suspected that this wasn't exactly the first year Evan hadn't had a Christmas tree in his living room. Determined to do it right, she'd gone out while he was at work and purchased ornaments, garlands and lights, all reduced to half price because it was so close to Christmas. Then they'd all gone out for the tree together. The slightly listing tree had been Libby's choice.

To preserve the untarnished image he seemed to have earned with Libby, Claire fell back on creativity. She figured a white lie was all right, as long as it was for a good cause.

"Because we're all going down to spend Christmas with his family and they have a big tree, so he thought maybe he wouldn't get one this year. Since he couldn't spend Christmas with it," she added when Libby looked at her pensively.

"Do you think our tree'll get lonely while we're gone?"

Libby had a heart as big as all outdoors, and Claire wouldn't have had it any other way. "Tell you what, when we get back, we'll have a little celebration for it and pretend it's Christmas all over again. The tree will never know the difference. What do you say?"

"All right!" Libby tugged on Claire's sweater. When Claire bent down, Libby pressed her lips to her cheek. "You're the best, Mama."

"What have I been telling you all along?" Claire laughed. She rose and saw Evan standing in the doorway. He had a strange, thoughtful expression on his face. Something was wrong. "What's the matter?"

Libby's excitement faded into the background. Claire knew he'd just taken a telephone call. They were leaving for Newport Beach early tomorrow morning—had plans been changed? Or had he changed his mind about their going with him after talking to his mother or someone else in the family?

Claire began to steel herself. Though she loved him and had agreed to marry him, Claire couldn't help keeping a little piece of herself in reserve, in case things didn't turn out the way she hoped. She was a dyed-in-the-wool optimist, but she was also a realist. Too many things had happened in her life for her not to be. The flip side of joy was sorrow.

The look on Evan's face had her bracing herself for an emotional blow. It was better to be ready than to be caught unprepared.

"That was Devin," he told her.

Evan looked at the tree. Signs of Libby's enthusiasm were lodged on various branches in the form of clumps of silver. His brother used to throw tinsel that way, he recalled, while he had meticulously laid strands out so that they hung down to catch the light. His were more artistic, but Devin's represented more fun. That's what had been missing in his life, he thought, before Claire. Fun.

He picked up a handful and threw it, just like Libby, surprising and pleasing Claire.

"He said he's coming by in a few minutes."

"Devin?" Claire didn't understand. "Isn't he with the rest of your family in Newport Beach?"

"Apparently not." He noticed there had been a strange, strained note in her voice. Evan looked at Claire and took her hand. It felt icy. The house wasn't cold. Was she getting ill again? Evan paused, trying to get his own feelings under control. "He's finally tracked down Rachel's mother."

The moment of respite disappeared, eaten up by concern. She couldn't read his eyes. What had Devin told him?

"Oh, God, Evan, is it bad news? Does she want Rachel back?"

Evan had been planning to file a petition with the court to get sole legal custody of Rachel. If her mother contested, Claire knew that at the very least, things could get ugly. And they could drag out for months, maybe even years. She didn't want that for the little girl, or for Evan.

Evan picked up another handful of tinsel; then, restless, he let it drop. "It was a bad connection. Devin said he'd tell me everything once he got here." Meanwhile, he thought, he was waiting, poised on the edge of razor-sharp pins.

He was worried; she could see it now. Any concerns of her own were pushed to the side. Evan needed her. Her hand closed over his.

"It'll be all right, Evan. If she wants Rachel back, we'll give her one hell of a fight," she said fiercely. "It's not so cut-and-dried anymore. More fathers are getting custody of their children these days, and she did abandon Rachel."

Evan wasn't saying anything. Maybe she had misread his expression. Maybe he was wrestling with his conscience, struggling with ambivalent feelings.

Claire lowered her voice so that Libby couldn't hear. "You do want her, don't you?"

She could ask that of him? In the beginning, sure, but now? He'd had the baby in his life just over six weeks, and it seemed like a lifetime. A frenzied, sweet lifetime. He'd dispensed with the idea of a nanny and left Rachel with Claire during the day. Every night he'd come home—not late, not with more work in his briefcase—but home to Rachel. To all of them. He couldn't picture his life the way it had once been and didn't want to.

"I want Rachel as much as I want to go on breathing." He looked at Claire, touching her cheek. "Almost as much as I want you."

She came to him then, wrapping her arms around his waist and pressing her face against his chest. Claire didn't want him to see the tears. Men didn't understand tears of joy. To them, tears always meant pain. If there was a pain in her heart, it was a sweet pain that she cherished.

"Well, then prepare yourself to go on breathing, Evan Quartermain, because you've got us, all of us, and we're not about to go away." She saw Libby watching them, the display of emotion making her hesitate. Claire extended one arm toward her daughter. "Are we, Libby?"

The little girl shook her head, then wiggled in between them to share in the hug.

* * *

The door opened on the very first ring. It was almost as if, Devin thought, his brother had stood waiting behind the door. There was apprehension in Evan's eyes, but the greeting between them was warmer than any he could recall in recent years.

And along with the concern he saw in Evan's eyes was something familiar. Something he'd seen in his own eyes in the mirror of late. Contentment.

"So how's it going?" Devin asked, taking his jacket off. Coming from the southern region of the state, he wasn't accustomed to this kind of cold weather and he hated the bulk of heavy clothing.

"You tell me." Should he be calling his lawyer, alerting him to prepare for a fight? Evan searched his brother's face for a clue.

Devin laughed shortly, still amazed at what a small world it was at times. "You know, it's the damnedest thing. That case I told you I was working on?" He'd given Evan no particulars, only that he had been devoting all his time to one case. But he had promised to find a way to look for Rachel's mother even if it meant giving up sleep. For Devin, it had been tantamount to an oath sworn in blood, since sleep had always been so important to him. "The trail wound up leading practically to your door. Next door, as a matter of fact." He jerked his thumb toward the other house. "Do you happen to know your neighbor?"

It was a legitimate question, Devin felt. Evan kept to himself and was, for the most part, oblivious to the people around him unless they somehow figured into his work.

Evan's eyebrows narrowed. What was Devin getting at? "Yes, intimately. Why?"

The word *intimately* stood out for Devin in large, flashing neon lights. So *that* was what was responsible for the change in his brother. My, God, he thought, truth was really stranger than fiction.

But before he had a chance to say anything further, their number increased by one.

Claire had hung back as long as decorum and patience had allowed. As well as being eager to meet his brother and see just how far the resemblance went, she was anxious to hear about Rachel's mother.

She walked in, her hand extended to Devin. "Hello, you must be Devin. I'm—"

"Claire Walker." Devin stared at her in amazement. If he hadn't just spoken to her on the telephone, he would have sworn that Blair had flown up here just to play a trick on him. "My, God, you look just like her. Exactly like her."

"Like who?" Claire looked to Evan for an explanation, but he merely lifted his shoulders in a confused shrug. "And how did you know my name?"

"Mama, did Evan split in half?" Libby crept hesitantly toward her mother, her eyes riveted to the man who looked just like Evan.

"No, honey, this is his twin brother, Devin," Claire replied uncertainly. Had Evan told his brother about her? That would explain how he knew her name, but who was the "her" he was referring to?

"I think you'd all better sit down for this," Devin told them. He knew *he* needed to.

Evan had no intention of dragging this out. "Devin, can we dispense with the dramatics and just have you tell me about Rachel's mother?"

That seemed almost like small potatoes now, although Devin knew that it meant a great deal to Evan. That in itself was a surprise. Their last conversation had been a complete reversal of the first. Rather than being eager to locate Rachel's mother so that he could give her back the baby, Evan now wanted him to make sure she was giving up all claim to the child. If anyone would have asked Devin, he would have said his brother had fallen under a spell. Now that he saw Claire, it all became clear to him.

"Everything's fine," Devin assured him. "She was really surprised you bothered having her traced, and even more surprised that you wanted sole custody of Rachel. But she meant what she said. She just wasn't cut out to be the mother type. She gave me all of Rachel's papers, birth certificate, record of immunizations, those kinds of things, and signed over custody to you. She just wants to have Rachel taken care of and to be free to go on with her own life."

Devin took out a bulging envelope from his jacket pocket, handing it over to Evan. He couldn't take his eyes off Claire. There was absolutely no difference between the woman beside Evan and the one he had left behind at home.

Evan opened the envelope and read the document. Only then did it sink in. Relief washed over him. This was far better than he'd hoped. Rachel was his without a fight; it was legal and binding. Claire was his, and soon that would be legal and binding, as well. They'd decided on a Valentine's Day wedding. He was getting a wife and two kids—and maybe a van to use on vacations. Evan couldn't remember when he had been happier.

Putting the papers back in the envelope, he looked at his brother. He knew Claire was beautiful, but Devin was staring at her as if she were an apparition.

"Now, what's this other thing you were talking about?" Evan slipped his arm protectively around Claire's shoulders. "Just how does Claire figure into your case?"

Devin laughed softly to himself. Wait till Evan heard about this! "Claire *is* my case."

"What?" Claire didn't understand. How could she be his case when she'd never met him before?

If he began in the beginning, it would take too long to

get to the point. Devin hopped to the middle. "Ms. Walker, do you know that you're adopted?"

An uneasy feeling began to creep through her. Claire nodded. "Yes, my father told me just before he died that he and my mother adopted me when I was about two years old." And then it came to her, riding on a bolt of lightning. "Is this about my sister?"

Libby urgently tugged on the edge of her sweater. "You have a sister, Mama?"

Her arm went around Libby, as if to shield her from any shock. "A twin."

It only confused Libby more. "Did you split in half, too, Mama?"

"No, honey, that's not how twins happen—exactly." She didn't have time to explain it to her now. As Claire looked at Devin, something twisted inside her chest, pricked by anxiety. "Is it about her?" she asked again in a whisper. She was vaguely aware that Evan's arm had tightened around her shoulders.

He nodded. "She didn't know about you until just recently. She found a photograph of the two of you with your mother—your birth mother—among her adoptive mother's things after she died. According to the back of the photograph, you were twenty-three months old. She'd been trying to locate you ever since."

Claire could feel herself trembling as joy, sorrow and confusion mixed in disproportionate measures within her. Part of her almost felt that this wasn't real. And yet, hadn't she always known? Even before Dr. Richmond had told her about her twin, hadn't something within her always felt that there was a piece of her that was missing?

"And my birth mother?" She wasn't even fully conscious of forming the words.

He hated being the bearer of bad news, but at least it was tempered with good, Devin thought. "Died a long time ago, I'm afraid. Of cancer. That was why you were put up for adoption,'' he explained quickly. He knew how much this had mattered to Blair. ''She didn't have anyone to care for the two of you.''

So it wasn't a case of abandonment, Claire thought as tears crept from the corners of her eyes and spilled down her cheeks. She'd been loved, not deserted like Rachel. She felt Evan leaning in to her and, for a moment, she grasped at the comfort he silently offered.

Claire drew in a large breath, then let it out slowly. She was in control again. ''When can I meet her?''

Devin walked out of the den, closing the doors behind him. Not that, knowing Blair, they would remain that way. He just wanted a moment to set the stage. It had taken him two days to get everything prepared. He'd done what he had intended to do beforehand. He'd asked Blair to marry him, and she had said yes. A yes that hadn't been borne on the tailwind of an emotional charge, something he knew was about to happen.

She'd said yes because she loved him as much as he had come to love her. As much as, he could see, Evan and Claire loved each other.

Now he was going to give Blair the gift he'd wanted to give her all along. They'd met when she'd hired him to find her sister. Things had quickly escalated between them, and though he had never mixed business with his private life before, this time he'd been helpless to prevent it. He made amends for that. He'd just given her back her retainer, leaving her to wonder if that meant that he was giving up the search for Claire.

She should have known him better than that, he mused, going out to the car. But she would. They had a lifetime before them to learn about each other's habits and traits, small and large.

He was rather looking forward to the learning process.

They were outside the car, waiting for him. Evan was holding the baby in his arms while Libby clutched Claire's hand. Devin grinned. He was never going to get used to the sight of his brother holding a baby, or the idea that Evan was a family man. It was something he was going to have to work on.

"C'mon," he beckoned. "I left her waiting in the den. Knowing her, we have about half a minute left to surprise her."

His hand on Claire's shoulder, Devin ushered her into the house. It was actually more of a mansion, he thought, and it belonged to Blair's aunt Beth. It was where the family, their numbers now large, congregated for holidays and celebrations. Behind them, he heard Evan telling Libby to remain with him. They all knew that this moment belonged to the two sisters who had been separated for twenty-two years.

"You'll be with her in a few minutes, I promise," Evan said, his voice patient.

Libby pouted, but did as she was told. She had come to trust Evan almost as much as she trusted her own mother. Mama had told her that they were all getting married and Evan was going to be her daddy. Mama was right, she thought with glee. Dreams did come true if you hoped hard enough.

Claire walked in uncertainly, anticipation making each breath she drew shallow. There were people in the house, people smiling at her. Some of the younger ones were staring unabashedly, awed by the resemblance between her and Blair, someone who had always been in their lives.

Blair's family. Blair had a family, Claire thought. That had to be such a wonderful feeling. Devin had filled her in on Blair's life as much as he could on the way down from San Francisco. Her twin had grown up believing she was an only child, just the way Claire had. But unlike hers, Blair's adoptive mother had a myriad of brothers and sisters. There had always been a house full of cousins for Blair to share her life with.

Claire felt envious, but happy that at least one of them had had a full, rich life.

No one was saying a word as they watched her pass. It was almost eerie.

And then she saw her.

Saw the woman who looked just like her. Her other half. Blair was staring at her, disbelief in her eyes.

And suddenly, Claire remembered a fragment that had haunted her younger years. She remembered there being a little girl who had looked just like her sitting beside her on the floor. She'd thought she'd dreamed it, imagined it, gotten a mirror mixed in with reality. Things like that happen when you're very young.

But it hadn't been a dream or a mirror. There had actually been someone else. Someone with her face, her eyes, her hair.

The other half of her.

And then suddenly, they were together again, two halves of a whole, sobbing and talking as they fell into each other's arms.

"I didn't think you were real," Claire cried, framing Blair's face between her hands. Her vision blurred. She blinked away the tears. "I thought I made you up."

"I had the same thought," Blair said excitedly. "But you're here, you're really here." How would she ever be able to thank Devin for finding her sister? There didn't seem to be a way. "Did he tell you?" Blair asked suddenly. "Devin? Did Devin tell you about our mother?"

Emotions choking her, Claire couldn't speak, only nod.

Blair wanted to be sure that Claire knew everything, that she wasn't tormented by feeling that she had been abandoned, the way she had believed herself to be. "That she didn't just give us away because we were inconvenient? That she loved us?"

It had meant so much to Blair to find that out, to know that she had been loved from the very beginning. She wanted Claire to know that, too, to have the same secure feeling that had finally come into her grasp.

"Yes, he told me everything." Claire's voice was hoarse as she tried to clear away the tears scratching along her throat.

Libby finally broke away from Evan and dashed to her mother, then stopped short as she looked from one woman to the other.

"Mama?" she said uncertainly. At least, it looked like Mama. She had on the same clothes and she smiled at her the same way, but what if she was wrong?

Claire knelt down beside her daughter and hugged her. That was when Libby knew it was all right.

Rising again, Claire placed her hands on Libby's shoulders and ushered the girl before her. "Libby, I'd like you to meet your aunt Blair."

Blair bent down to be closer to Libby's level. "Hello, Libby. How are you?"

Libby couldn't help staring. "You have Mama's face." She wasn't sure she understood all this. Was this magic? Or were they all on TV? "And he has Evan's." She looked at Devin, her eyes growing huge again. "Are you outer-space people?"

Laughing, Evan came forward. He shifted Rachel to his other shoulder. "I think that might be my fault. I let her watch an old 'Star Trek' episode with me the other night. I was exposing her to science," he explained, answering the question in Claire's eyes. "The captain split in half during a malfunction in the transporter room. I think Libby thinks we might have visited a transporter room."

Tickled, Blair laughed as she ruffled her new niece's hair. "No, honey, we're not from outer space—we're from Newport Beach. And we're your family." Blair slipped her arm around Claire's shoulder. "From here on in."

Devin could only shake his head as he looked around him at his brother, the two women in their lives and the two children.

"Wait until Ma sees all of us." Devin chucked Rachel under the chin, and she gurgled, drooling down Evan's shoulder. "This is going to be one heck of a Merry Christmas for her."

Claire looked at her sister as both their eyes filled with tears again.

"For all of us," she amended.

And then the ranks closed in around them. Blair's extended family had decided, as one, that they had given the new arrivals enough time together. Now it was their turn to get acquainted.

Converging, they assimilated all six into their midst.

Epilogue

Blair eased herself into the tiny vestibule just off to the side of the church entrance where, only a short month ago, she had been the one dressed in the long, lacy wedding gown. Now her sister was wearing it for her wedding. They had decided to use the same one for luck, beginning a tradition.

Their very first, but not, Blair knew, their last.

It had been less than two months since they had first hugged and cried after a twenty-two-year separation, and they were already deeply entrenched in each other's lives. They spoke on the phone every day, sometimes two or three times. Devin claimed they were making the long-distance phone company rich, but Claire and Blair both knew how pleased he was that he had been instrumental in bringing them together.

Claire looked absolutely gorgeous. Had she looked that radiant when she had worn the gown? Blair wondered with affection.

"We've got a packed house," Blair told her sister. She fussed a little with the veil. "Are you ready?"

Claire let out a deep breath, then smiled at her twin. Sometimes, even after all these weeks, she still woke up in the morning and thought it was all just a wonderful dream. But it wasn't. It was real. All of it. Evan, Rachel. Blair. All real.

"I think I've been ready for this all my life." Happiness and affection outlined her face. "Thanks for lending me your uncle."

Blair shrugged it off. No words of thanks were necessary between them. "You needed something borrowed." The gown was technically now something old; she'd given Claire a blue garter to wear, and as for something new, Evan had given her a stunning necklace in the shape of a heart, encrusted with diamonds. Claire was all set. "Besides, he's not my uncle, he's *our* uncle." Blair gave her sister a light squeeze. "What's mine is yours—you know that."

There was a light rap on the door. When Blair opened it, Uncle John peered in. Blair grinned. "Speak of the devil."

Uncle John raised gray tufted brows in mock affront. "Is that any way to talk about your old uncle? Although your aunt does say I still have a little devil in my eye." He chuckled wickedly. And then he looked at Claire and sighed. She was the picture of happiness, just as Blair had been in her place. "You know, with you ladies using the same dress, this feels like déjà vu for me. Especially since the guy waiting at the altar looks the same." He shook his head. He'd never seen two men look more alike. "Beats me how you're going be able to tell them apart." He glanced at Blair, a smile quirking his mouth. "You might consider tagging their right ear, like they do with animals in the wild."

Claire laughed. She could just picture that, although a

single small gold hoop dangling from his ear might be sexy on Evan at that.

"We can tell them apart, Uncle John," Blair assured him with a grin. "Devin's smile is lopsided."

"And Evan's the one with baby drool on his shoulder," Claire added. And she couldn't think of anything more endearing to her than that. It attested to just how much he cared for his daughter. How much he would care for a child of their own when the time came.

"How're you going to tell them apart once Rachel's older?" Uncle John asked.

"I'll think of something," Claire promised, her eyes shining.

Blair held up her hand, stopping any further exchange, as she cocked her head, listening. The organist had begun playing the song they had agreed upon to precede "The Wedding March." This was it.

She looked at Claire. "I think they're playing our song."

Uncle John puffed up his chest. "Well, ladies, shall we?" He offered his arm to Claire. "You know, I'm really going to miss this. Know anyone we can marry off next month?"

"We'll look into it," Blair told him. Moving past her uncle, Blair brushed her sister's cheek with her lips for luck, then lowered the veil over Claire's face. She stood back and, surveying her handiwork, nodded. "Perfect."

This time, she thought as she opened the door, she would get to be the observer and, in a way, see what her wedding had been like. Last month, her stomach in a tight knot, she had gone through the entire ceremony in a complete blur.

Outside the room, Blair gathered with the other bridesmaids and ushers. It was a mix of her family, Evan's and Claire's friends. Six couples in all. Devin was waiting for her at the altar, standing beside Evan, just as Evan had stood beside him last month.

She was still more nervous, she thought, than Claire, even though this was her sister's wedding, not hers. Those same butterflies, slightly smaller in size, were back in her stomach.

They grew a little as the organist began "The Wedding March" with gusto, filling the already packed church with music. Blair watched the others move down the aisle two by two. And then it was her turn. She looked over her shoulder and winked at Claire. Her sister looked absolutely radiant. Not a trace of nerves anywhere. She supposed that was her job.

"Meet you up front," she whispered to Claire. Taking a deep breath, she began the slow, rhythmic walk down the aisle.

"Nervous?" Uncle John asked.

Claire shook her head ever so slightly, careful not to dislodge her headpiece. "No, excited."

It felt like fireworks were going off in her veins. Wonderful fireworks. Claire saw the trail of flower petals strewed all down the aisle. There were handfuls clumped here and there. Libby's handiwork. She and one of Blair's youngest nieces were her flower girls. Claire's mouth curved as she remembered Libby bragging that she was getting really good at throwing flowers. Libby was eager for the next wedding. With a family this large, there was bound to be another one soon.

Claire's smile widened as she walked beside Uncle John. Toward Evan. He looked so handsome, standing there, she thought. Her heart swelled, knowing she had finally found everything she had ever been looking for.

And to think, unbeknownst to her, it had all started out with a search for Blair. For in Blair's search to find her,

Claire knew her sister had found herself, as well. And they had found one another and enough happiness in between to more than fill two lives.

*   *   *   *   *

Don't miss Devin and Blair's story!
Look for
DESPERATELY SEEKING TWIN...
available this month only from
Silhouette Yours Truly.

Take 4 bestselling love stories FREE

Plus get a FREE surprise gift!

Special Limited-time Offer

Mail to Silhouette Reader Service™

3010 Walden Avenue
P.O. Box 1867
Buffalo, N.Y. 14240-1867

YES! Please send me 4 free Silhouette Romance™ novels and my free surprise gift. Then send me 6 brand-new novels every month, which I will receive months before they appear in bookstores. Bill me at the low price of $2.67 each plus 25¢ delivery and applicable sales tax, if any.* That's the complete price and a savings of over 10% off the cover prices—quite a bargain! I understand that accepting the books and gift places me under no obligation ever to buy any books. I can always return a shipment and cancel at any time. Even if I never buy another book from Silhouette, the 4 free books and the surprise gift are mine to keep forever.

215 BPA A3UT

Name	(PLEASE PRINT)	
Address	Apt. No.	
City	State	Zip

This offer is limited to one order per household and not valid to present Silhouette Romance™ subscribers. *Terms and prices are subject to change without notice. Sales tax applicable in N.Y.

USROM-696   ©1990 Harlequin Enterprises Limited

Welcome to the Towers!

In January
New York Times bestselling author

NORA ROBERTS

takes us to the fabulous Maine coast mansion
haunted by a generations-old secret and introduces
us to the fascinating family that lives there.

Mechanic Catherine "C.C." Calhoun and hotel magnate
Trenton St. James mix like axle grease and mineral
water—until they kiss. Efficient Amanda Calhoun finds
easygoing Sloan O Riley insufferable—and irresistible.
And they all must race to solve the mystery
surrounding a priceless hidden emerald necklace.

Catherine and Amanda

THE Calhoun Women

**A special 2-in-1 edition containing
COURTING CATHERINE and A MAN FOR AMANDA.**

Look for the next installment of
THE CALHOUN WOMEN with Lilah and Suzanna's
stories, coming in March 1998.

Available at your favorite retail outlet.

Silhouette®

As seen on TV!
Free Gift Offer

With a Free Gift proof-of-purchase from any Silhouette® book, you can receive a beautiful cubic zirconia pendant.

This gorgeous marquise-shaped stone is a genuine cubic zirconia—accented by an 18" gold tone necklace.

(Approximate retail value $19.95)

Send for yours today...
compliments of ▼ *Silhouette*®
TM

To receive your free gift, a cubic zirconia pendant, send us one original proof-of-purchase, photocopies not accepted, from the back of any Silhouette Romance™, Silhouette Desire®, Silhouette Special Edition®, Silhouette Intimate Moments® or Silhouette Yours Truly™ title available at your favorite retail outlet, together with the Free Gift Certificate, plus a check or money order for $1.65 U.S./$2.15 CAN. (do not send cash) to cover postage and handling, payable to Silhouette Free Gift Offer. We will send you the specified gift. Allow 6 to 8 weeks for delivery. Offer good until December 31, 1997, or while quantities last. Offer valid in the U.S. and Canada only.

Free Gift Certificate

Name: _____

Address: _____

City: _____ State/Province: _____ Zip/Postal Code: _____

Mail this certificate, one proof-of-purchase and a check or money order for postage and handling to: SILHOUETTE FREE GIFT OFFER 1997. In the U.S.: 3010 Walden Avenue, P.O. Box 9077, Buffalo NY 14269-9077. In Canada: P.O. Box 613, Fort Erie, Ontario L2Z 5X3.

FREE GIFT OFFER   084-KFD
ONE PROOF-OF-PURCHASE
To collect your fabulous FREE GIFT, a cubic zirconia pendant, you must include this
original proof-of-purchase for each gift with the properly completed Free Gift Certificate.

084-KFDR